D1741786

THE HOUSE OF
NIGHTINGALES

THE HOUSE OF NIGHTINGALES

SUZANNE EBEL

SEVERN HOUSE PUBLISHERS

This first world edition published in 1985 by
SEVERN HOUSE PUBLISHERS LTD of
4 Brook Street, London W1Y 1AA

Copyright © Suzanne Ebel, 1985

British Library Cataloguing in Publication Data
Ebel, Suzanne
   The house of nightingales
   I. Title
   823'.914[F]   PR6057.0585
   ISBN 0 7278 1160 6

All rights reserved. Unauthorised duplication
contravenes applicable laws.

Typeset by Inforum Ltd, Portsmouth, England
Printed and bound by Butler & Tanner Ltd,
Frome, England

1

The telephone rang while Holly was in the garden. She disentangled her fingers from a rose briar, ran up the path and through the french windows. It was sure to be Mike.

Picking up the receiver she said, 'Don't tell me, let me guess! You want to bring someone round again this evening!'

There was a moment's silence and an unfamiliar voice with a French accent, sounding puzzled, said, 'May I speak to Madame St Martin?'

'That's me.' Holly hoped the foreign voice would hurry up. Mike had recently thought up this idea of inviting clients to meet him at her house for drinks sometimes. Occasionally one of them rang to check her address.

'My name is Deslauriers,' said the voice, 'I'm a friend of your parents-in-law at Vanergues.'

She was very surprised. What on earth could *they* want?

'I have a message from them. I wonder if I might call to see you?'

'Of course. Any time. How kind,' she hastily added, suddenly understanding the mystery. A present must be on its way for Miranda's birthday.

The stranger said that if it was convenient he

could come at six this evening, and yes, he knew her Richmond address. When he rang off, Holly returned to the garden. Cutting dead heads from a big bush of yellow roses, she was thoughtful. She didn't know exactly why that telephone call had slightly disturbed her. Why should it? People coming to England often delivered parcels from friends living abroad. The girl next door had a sister in Spain, and bulky parcels arrived at Christmas or for birthdays, delivered by an obliging Spanish friend coming to London on business. It was nothing out of the ordinary for presents to arrive in this way. But there was a big difference between a present for her neighbour from Spain, and the one now on its way from France. Holly had never met her parents-in-law. They were complete strangers.

The St Martins were French, as Holly's husband had been; they owned a fashionable hotel called La Maison des Rossignols, the House of Nightingales, in Provence. For her stepdaughter's birthday, the French grandparents sent boring cards which arrived late. The cards, with *Meilleurs Voeux* lettered in gritty bits of silver, contained messages using formal French words. 'To our grand-daughter Miranda, kindest souvenirs.' 'Affectionate greetings from your Grandparents.' 'Our sincere thoughts.' Things like that. It was odd how you couldn't send love in French.

Finishing with the rose bush, Holly sat down on the grass. It was bone dry after a week of sunshine. She put her arms round her knees, and looked round at the green hand of summer.

The garden was long and narrow, and somebody fifty years ago had trained shrubs so skilfully that all

2

the walls were now covered; it could almost have been a country garden. There were clematis and honeysuckle, syringa, climbing roses. Miranda, who was nine, liked to picnic out here, and often wheedled Holly into taking their trays out of doors. They'd even eaten in the garden on dry days in winter. Food, declared Miranda, always tasted different in the open.

It was at this time of early summer two years before, when Holly and Miranda were in the garden, that the foreign telegram had come. Robert, her husband and Miranda's father, had been killed in a plane crash on the other side of the world. Even now, the memory had an extraordinary unreality. Robert had been in the Far East, working on his new book. She and Miranda had both received a few postcards; he never wrote either of them a letter.

Knowing he was alive had been like hearing a continuous piece of music. It was true that the melodies hadn't been particularly happy, but they'd played all the time. Robert, said the music, was thousand of miles away but he would come back to them both, to his wife and his daughter. They would see him again. When Holly opened the telegram, the music, with a dreadful grinding sound, came to a brutal stop.

Being a widow was a strange thing when one was only twenty-five. Holly's friends thought that, and so did she. The word seemed to Holly to describe a woman of mature age who had led a full and happy life. Perhaps she had children who were grown-up now. Her past must surely be rich in blessings of all she had known and shared and learned and treasured. 'Widow' was a word of dignity and

3

fulfilment as well as sorrow.

But Holly had been nineteen when she married, and she had lost her husband just four years later. He disappeared from her life without a word, leaving her the care of his daughter, the house with the long garden – and a haunting knowledge that he had never really loved her.

Holly had been a thin, leggy girl with a coltish, gawky look. Her dark hair was short and feathery, her pretty nose slightly snub. Her eyes were grey. They could burn with interest sometimes. She had an expressive, perhaps too expressive face.

'Learn to hide your feelings, my child,' her mother used to say. Holly declared she'd rather not hide them at all, because *she* believed feelings should show. Her mother shook her head and laughed. Her only child's theories, stories, friends, plans, amused her. Mother and daughter lived in a cottage in Kent ten minutes from the sea. When Holly went to university she still managed to live at home. Other girls in her year eagerly escaped their families, lived in college and merrily threw parental care and opinions over the windmill. Holly didn't. She and her mother were almost like an elder and younger sister. Holly's father had left them when she was very small, neither she nor her mother had seen him again. Later he had died. So Holly and her mother only had each other.

Her mother's health was not robust and by the time Holly was in her mid-teens she had begun coping with any domestic problems. They had little money, but were never bored. When they sat up late watching American blockbusters on TV, Holly would exclaim, 'Quick! Tell me what happens!' and rush out to get the coffee. They made each other laugh. They talked about everything in the world. It was as if their conversation, begun in Holly's childhood, was something unending which rippled and flowed like a bright river. Holly did not look elsewhere for a close friend. She sometimes wondered now if she had known, in a mysterious, instinctive way, that she was not destined to have her mother for long.

Swerving away from the memory of her mother's death, Holly thought about the time when she'd first met Robert St Martin. He had come into her life when her mother was ill. St Martin was a novelist with a big reputation, who wrote intensely exciting books set in distant places. He wrote of murders in Greenland, archeological thefts in Bali, stories of espionage and danger and what he described as 'the crime and the punishment'. He was giving a series of lectures on The Modern Novel in Europe at the university when Holly was in her third term. She went to one of the lectures and was intrigued.

'The great man,' said Emma, a girl in her year, 'wants to meet you.'

'Emma, what rubbish!'

'But it's true,' said Emma who liked to tease. 'Robert St Martin is a friend of my parents. I said hello to him last night after the lecture, and he asked who was the dark girl sitting next to me. Obviously he'd noticed you were riveted. Would you like to meet him?'

Holly wanted to refuse, she thought it embarrassing. But after the next lecture Emma dashed up to Robert St Martin, dragged him over to Holly and introduced them with a flourish.

'Here's your great fan, Robert!'

She then went to join her boyfriend, leaving them together.

Holly and Robert St Martin gave each other polite smiles. Both looked somewhat wry, and conversation to begin with was forced. He was a heavily built man with a long face, and a mouth which turned up at the corners. This gave him a deceptively amusing look – he had little sense of humour. He was very pleasant to the young girl who was clearly impressed. His manner was kind and, in the way of celebrities, somewhat grand. To Holly's surprise, as talk grew easier, he asked her out for a drink. She often wondered later why she had confided in him that evening. She was not a person who spoke of her private worries to strangers, it was one of the things about her that was not impulsive. But St Martin was older than any of her friends – in his thirties and seeming more. He was a consequential, serious man, and *he* confided to her that his life was not what it had been. His wife had recently died. She was filled with sympathy and strong fellow-feeling when he told her that, and it was then that she spoke about her mother's illness. He'd been so kind to her. So concerned. He had a fellow-feeling too.

When her mother grew worse and had to go to hospital, Robert was constantly in touch with Holly. He came to university to fetch her and drive her to the hospital. He waited in corridors, took her out to meals, telephoned her every day. When her mother died, it was Robert who arranged the funeral. Holly had no relatives.

St Martin lived in Richmond-on-Thames, in the house he had bought when he married and where he, his wife Sally and their child had lived until Sally's death. Now he lived there alone with his daughter. At the end of term he invited Holly to spend a day at Richmond.

Holly never forgot the first time she saw Miranda. It was early December and bitterly cold. The child, who was about four, was being minded by a neighbour who told them she was in the garden. Holly and Robert went to the french windows. There, at the end of the garden, a small figure in a coat with a hood was crouched over a flower bed, digging with bare hands in earth that was rock solid. Holly went out and knelt on the frosty grass. The child looked round. Her face was pale with cold.

'Hello, I'm Holly.'

'My name's Miranda.'

'Shall we go in and make some toast?'

Standing up, Miranda allowed Holly to take her hand.

She was an elfish child who did not look in the least like her mother, whose fashionable painting hung in the sitting room. Sally St Martin had been attractive in an actressy way, with stylish blonde hair and high cheekbones. Miranda did not resemble her father either, except that they both had brown eyes. He was heavily built, heavy-featured, with a serious, slow manner. The child was skinny and sallow, she had an infectious grin. She was fidgety, and found it hard to keep still. Her hair was an odd mixture of blonde and brown – Holly said it was striped.

The child had been quite friendly, but much too quiet when Holly first met her. She was a mouse of a thing. But as the winter went by and Holly often came to the Richmond house, she noticed that

Miranda was beginning to sing to herself, to hop about, and that she often laughed. When Holly left for her train, Miranda used to say, 'When are you coming again?'

In the early spring, Robert and Holly were married.

Sitting in the garden now, hearing the drone of a plane coming into London, Holly thought of her husband with an ache of the heart. How different her marriage had been from what she'd hoped and believed. Nothing had been right except Miranda.

Robert wasn't putting on an act when he and Holly first met, and he'd been so concerned and kind during the dreadful months of her mother's final illness. He had brought her to Richmond to meet his little daughter. He had gently kissed her. Eventually, he had asked her to be his wife. He was a good man, in his way. But it had been an arm's length way. Browning wrote: 'God be thanked the meanest of his creatures Boasts two soul-side, one to face the world with, One to show a woman when he loves her.' Holly's husband never showed her his other soul-side. That had belonged to Miranda's mother and he couldn't give his heart away a second time. Sally had been clever, beautiful, full of personality, a successful journalist admired for her strong opinions and writing style. In the portrait she leaned forward, half laughing. Sometimes Holly thought she saw something penetrating in the painted blue eyes.

'Sally was quite brilliant,' Robert often remarked. He would sigh over some article in the newspapers. 'Now *she* would have known how to handle this subject.'

'Sally was all set to have a TV series.'

'Sally thought my last book would make a superb movie. She wanted to try her hand at the script.'

Her name echoed through Holly's life. Robert couldn't forget her. When Holly had promised to love and honour him, when she became Miranda's second mother, she had never guessed she was marrying Yesterday.

All that was behind her now. She and Miranda lived here in the Richmond house as happily as she'd lived with her own mother. In the same way, they shared things. They played ping-pong on the dining-room table, and Miranda had begun to win. They discussed clothes – Miranda had strong opinions. They talked about homework, pop music, what plants they wanted in the garden. In the last two years life had settled into a pattern of love and youth.

Now, suddenly, out of the blue, the past was reasserting itself. Robert's French parents were making a move towards them. Holly couldn't rid herself of the uneasy feeling that something wasn't quite right.

It was already half-past five, and her visitor was due soon. Holly would have to meet him alone. This evening Miranda had an hour's swimming; she was good at sports and was being coached for the Junior swimming gala. So there would be no Miranda to brighten the occasion.

Going up to her room, Holly looked at herself somewhat dubiously in the long mirror. She was wearing a white knitted-cotton dress striped in lilac and blue, with a broad belt. It suited her. But it was three years old and nobody could say it had style. 'Why do I think I've got to look stylish just because this Frenchman's calling round?' she thought. 'I suppose he'll be rich and middle-aged like the St Martins. Well, he'll just have to put up with me as I am.'

She went down to the sitting room. The house to which Robert had brought her when they married, and where she'd signally failed to replace for him the ghost of Sally St Martin, was pleasantly old fashioned. The comfortable furniture was covered in blue-and-white chintz; Robert's books – he'd had literally thousands – reached to the ceiling on shelves built on three sides of the room. One needed library steps to get to the top shelves. When Holly first came to the house, she thought it exactly like the home of a university tutor. There was that lived-in, cosy, shabby, bookish atmosphere. She hadn't imagined an internationally famous writer and his journalist wife would create a home like that. She was right. Robert told her later that he had bought the house literally lock, stock and barrel, with all its furniture and fittings, from a couple who were leaving to work in New York. Only the books and pictures were Robert's.

Holly was much amused at the idea of buying a home ready made. But Robert saw nothing unusual about that.

'It saved time and Sally was as busy as I was. Besides, she wasn't interested in domesticity. You know how it often is with intellectual women.' In his face was the expression he wore only when speaking of his lost wife.

The unpretentious comfort of the house suited Holly. She enjoyed cooking in the kitchen, which had a door into a small conservatory where a vine grew, pressing broad leaves against the glass. Its grapes were very sour, so she and Miranda made them into jelly. She liked the sitting room, the library steps, the french windows which, as she walked into the room this evening, were still wide. The scent of a great bush of syringa came floating in with its tang of oranges.

The travelling clock on the mantelpiece said six. The bell rang at exactly that moment and, although she'd been expecting it, she gave a slight jump.

A man was standing at the front door. Holly looked at him with a feeling of quite ludicrous surprise. Where was the short, grizzled Frenchman she'd seen so clearly in her mind? The one with a large parcel under his arm? Her visitor was tall, olive-skinned and no more than thirty. He gave a half bow.

'Madame St Martin?'

Holly disliked 'Madame', it sounded so elderly.

'Yes. Do come in.'

'It's good of you to see me at such short notice.'

He followed her into the sitting room. The sun was turning the garden into a deeper gold, the lawn was patterned with long shadows.

'What a lovely room,' he said.

Holly smiled and asked him to sit down, offering him a choice of white wine or sherry.

'Sherry would be nice, thank you. In France, you know, we haven't yet adopted the English habit of drinking wine as an aperitif.'

His English, with its attractive accent, was remarkably good. But Holly didn't care if French people drank wine before supper or not; she poured the sherry.

They began to talk as strangers do, laying facts

11

down like playing a children's game of cards. How long had she lived in Richmond? Did she like the district? What hotel was he staying at? Did he often visit London? While the somewhat artificial conversation went on, she looked at him curiously. Married to a Frenchman for five years, she had never known any other French person but her husband. Robert had no friends among his own countrymen, never visited France even to take Holly and his daughter to meet his parents. A mystery about him was the way he completely rejected his country. Yet France had made him: created the way he looked, the way he thought, the way he was. And it had coloured his voice, as it coloured Paul Deslauriers', with entrancing lilts and intonations.

Her visitor, though, was unlike Robert in everything but the accent. Robert's long face had been rather supercilious, Paul Deslauriers' was oval and lively. Her husband's heavy-lidded eyes had looked non-comittally out on to the world. This man's sparkled and he laughed easily. He had a boyish cast of feature, his nose short and straight, his black hair slightly curly. But he was very poised and confident.

'You sounded surprised when I rang,' he remarked, after a pause in the banalities.

'I suppose I was. Then I realised that the St Martins must have asked you to bring over Miranda's present.'

Even as she was speaking, she realised he wasn't carrying a parcel. Had he left it at his hotel?

It was his turn to look surprised.

'A present?'

'Why, yes, for her birthday last week – oh, goodness!'

She threw up her hands in embarrassment and burst out laughing. 'Oh dear, I am sorry! I really thought they'd decided to send her something this time. Do forgive me!'

She looked at him with guilty amusement, still laughing.

'I imagined they'd developed a conscience about her,' she added, not seeing why she shouldn't say it.

'*Of course* they should have sent something,' he exclaimed. 'Jacqueline would have enjoyed getting a present for the little girl. She loves shopping. What a lost opportunity! But I'm afraid I've come with empty hands. It's I who must apologise.'

'It doesn't matter a bit,' said Holly, still inclined to giggle. 'They've never sent her anything but a card before. Forget I said it, please.'

He sipped the sherry, remarking that sherry from Bristol was the best in the world. 'Oh, wouldn't he,' thought Holly. It was just the kind of thing one knew a Frenchman would say. She still felt amused.

'Something you said just now is quite true,' he said after a moment. 'The St Martins do have rather a guilty conscience about the grandchild they've never met.'

'Robert was always so busy,' said Holly. She had told the loyal lie many times before. 'That was why he didn't take her to France. I know he and his first wife, Sally, went to Provence to see his parents years ago, before they married. But later, I mean when I came on the scene, his time was completely taken up with work. He went all over the world to get his background material. He simply hadn't the opportunity to go to France again.'

Paul Deslauriers nodded politely. But he looked at

her with a somewhat penetrating glance from eyes as dark as Miranda's. Holly hoped he didn't hear in her voice or guess by her tiresomely transparent face, that she deeply disapproved of the in-laws she had never met. During her marriage she had disapproved of her husband *and* his parents for the unnatural way they behaved to each other.

When Robert first told her that he never went to see them she had actually laughed. Why, they must go to France as soon as possible and take Miranda with them! What could be simpler? But nothing was simple and Robert least of all. He wouldn't go. He scarcely wrote to his parents – a card now and then – and when she impulsively suggested writing them a long, newsy letter he said he preferred her not to do so. The breach was mysterious and permanent.

'So I've brought nothing with me, alas,' Paul Deslauriers said. 'But I have been asked to bring you a message. The St Martins are old friends of mine. As a matter of fact, I work for them.'

'At the hotel, the Maison des Rossignols?'

'At all three hotels.'

Holly did not realise that she made a rueful face.

'You don't approve?' he said. 'You don't like the idea of three hotels instead of just the one. They're very attractive and well run, I promise.'

'That wasn't what I was thinking,' she said hastily. 'I just feel rather stupid at knowing so little about my husband's family. Three hotels. I had no idea.'

'We're pleased that the St Martin's little empire, as Christian will call it, is growing,' he said pleasantly. 'He bought a hotel in Bavaria some years ago. His idea is to try and create the right atmosphere, com-

14

fort, pleasant places to eat and sleep. And first-rate food. You know the kind of thing.'

Holly, who knew nothing about first-class hotels, hoped that it didn't show. She nodded. More recently, added Paul Deslauriers, Christian had bought a hotel near Barcelona. Now there was the interesting possibility of one in England.

'That's one of the reasons I'm here. The other was the hope of meeting you. Jacqueline asked me to see if there was a chance we could meet. She's sent you a message.'

Holly smiled briefly, thinking how peculiar it was to receive a message from her mother-in-law after all this time. Her only knowledge of Madame St Martin, apart from the boring birthday cards, had been the letter of condolence when Robert was killed. It had been written in French of a chilling formality.

'It is the St Martin's fortieth wedding anniversary this August, there's going to be a great celebration. Many, many friends. Jacqueline told me to say how happy she and Christian will be if you and Miranda can come.'

Leaning forward, his elbows on his knees, he gave her a charming smile.

Holly looked at him blankly. 'To the Maison des Rossignols?'

'Yes. We're organising a really big party. It will be so nice to have you and the little girl among the guests.'

She paused. Then said slowly and carefully, 'It's very kind of them. I'm terribly sorry, but I'm afraid we can't come.'

'I'm sure you don't mean that.'

'I'm afraid I do.'

'But –'

'But when Miranda's term ends we are going straight to Kent. To a cottage by the sea. It's all arranged.'

Her manner was decidedly brusque and she knew it, but the invitation had annoyed her for some reason.

'Surely you could rearrange things?'

'No, we couldn't.'

Then, seeing the look on his face, she went on: 'In any case, it is much too expensive. Miranda and I couldn't fly out for a party! It's a wonderful idea,' continued Holly, not meaning it, 'but we couldn't afford it. Please thank them very much for us and say we appreciate the kind thought and – and let me give you some more sherry.'

She sprang up, glad to do something instead of watching the smile die out of his face.

He thanked her, said again that the sherry was very good and held his glass up to the light. 'Oh, do get back to the point,' thought Holly. She was uncomfortable. 'And then,' she thought with relief, 'you can go.'

'I'm afraid there's something you've misunderstood, madame.'

'Do you think you need to call me that?' she said in a more friendly way. 'We really *do* use Christian names right away in England and madame sounds so odd. Could you manage Holly? I was born in December,' she added, offering the fact as a small apology for her brusqueness.

'Thank you,' he said. And didn't call her madame or Holly either. 'There's something you've misunderstood and it's my fault, I put it badly. Jacqueline didn't invite you both merely to the party. That would have been absurd. She wants you to spend the summer with us at the Rossignols. She's eager to meet you and her grandchild, and so is Christian. I'm sure we could make you happy there.'

He looked at her expectantly for the second time.

She couldn't think of a word to say. The rich invitation was a shock, it almost staggered her. But instead of being pleased, she was more annoyed still. Who did these people think they were? They asked this young man to come and see her, calmly sending messages by him as if they were royalty and he a sort of ambassador. They expected her to pack up and set off with Miranda to stay in a strange country hundreds of miles away for no reason except that they'd suddenly thought of the idea. She and Miranda weren't expected to have plans of their own.

'How kind of them. But it's still out of the question, I'm afraid.' She was no actress, and her feelings showed.

'Surely —' began Paul Deslauriers when a voice shouted from the front door.

'You there, Petal?'

Mike Armstrong bustled in carrying two bottles of wine in a plastic bag. He drew up short when he saw Paul and raised enquiring eyebrows.

'You didn't say we were entertaining or I'd have brought another bottle. How do you do? The name's Armstrong.'

Holly introduced them and they shook hands.

Never at a loss, Mike fetched a corkscrew, opened a bottle of Beaujolais and plunged into breezy talk with the visitor.

17

Mike was a recent friend of Holly's, an estate agent who had met her at a party, and spent hours trying to persuade her to sell her house. He was a short, stocky young man with ginger hair and a freckled face which hid a shrewd, bustling nature under an ingenuous grin. He was the most energetic man Holly had ever met. When he realised that it was no use trying to talk her into selling the Richmond house, he appeared at her home with a bottle of wine and the suggestion that she might turn the house into two flats. 'We've loads of punters who want to live in your area.'

He asked her to look at other houses which had been successfully developed in this way. His business plans failed with her, but he took a fancy to her, and Mike certainly made her laugh. He took her out to supper. He fell into the habit of turning up, bringing a bottle of wine, and sharing bacon and eggs. He dashed in and out of her life, often bringing a client with him.

'You don't mind, as long as I provide the drink, do you, Petal?'

He also bought small presents for Miranda. But the little girl was offhand with him. Once he asked her to sit on his lap. 'What a silly idea,' she'd said.

It was true that Mike was too fond of money, too fixed on business, rarely talking of anything else, but he was energetic, lively, funny and young, and he admired Holly. She accepted his friendship and didn't take him seriously.

As he sat talking to Paul Deslauriers she saw how skilfully he discovered within a few minutes what Paul's work was; by the time Holly refilled his glass, he also knew that Paul was interested in buying an English hotel.

'Tell you what. Get in touch with me,' said Mike. 'Armstrong & Meredith. We're an up-and-coming firm, I assure you.' He laughed, showing his even teeth. 'Hotels are very much in our line.'

Paul Deslauriers was quite interested but Holly did wish that Mike wouldn't push: after all, he'd only just met the man. But Mike combined the energy of a jet engine with the hide of a rhinoceros, thought Holly, mixing her metaphors. Mike was talking too much, and Holly sat silent, thinking that Paul Deslauriers coped very well with all that salesmanship. Eventually he stood up and said he really must go.

Mike remained seated, waving a hand holding a wine glass. He repeated his telephone number and said not to forget to give him a buzz.

Holly and the visitor walked to the front door. As she opened it, he said quietly, 'Change your mind about coming to France.'

'It's a very generous invitation. But we can't. I'm sorry. Thank you for coming to see me.'

He hesitated, as if he wanted to say more. Then took her hand and briefly kissed it. The gesture was so casual and unexpected that Holly was taken by surprise.

Miranda was in high spirits during the following week. As her sports teacher had hoped, she won a medal at the Junior swimming gala. Holly sat with other parents by the swimming pool, to see her girl win by a few strokes, climbing out beaming and dripping.

The school was less than quarter of an hour away from the house, and Holly walked there with Miranda every morning and fetched her each evening unless the weather was very bad. Then Holly drove in the Mini. After the gala, on an evening of more sunshine, they walked home. Miranda hopped rather than walked.

'Did you notice, Holly, how I kicked really hard to get a good start? That's important, you know. And I thought I'd never get in front of Claudia but I did. *And* she's three months older than me.'

She was silent, but only for a minute.

'Do you see that sparrow? Can you tell a house sparrow from a hedge one? The house sparrow has a grey crown, see?'

Miranda liked to give information, particularly about her new enthusiasm, bird-watching. She was also good at spotting planes. 'I saw Concorde twice.' She enjoyed a variety of things: Mickey Mouse T-shirts, trampolining at school, writing poems, hamburgers, Asterix and painting large benign-looking crocodiles. She was nine years old.

She and Holly had been friends from the day Holly had seen her digging in the frosty garden. There were sixteen years between the child and the 'child bride' as her university friends had nicknamed Holly when she married. Holly had discovered something when she met Miranda – that it was possible to love instantly. From the moment she'd met her, Holly had loved the little girl with all her soul.

Robert had been pleased in a way. But once he had said, 'You take too much notice of her.' The impetuous reply, 'I am all she has,' was on the tip of Holly's tongue, but she swallowed it. It was true, but it was unkind. Robert hadn't been much interested in Miranda. Children bored him. It was Sally's idea to have a child and he'd agreed to make her happy. When Sally died, most of his affection for Miranda probably died too. Or was it, thought Holly, that he'd been a man who couldn't connect with the young. There were men like that – fathers only interested in their children as they were growing up. During the first years of her marriage Holly had already discovered that he was a man with flaws.

She had loved two people in her life and lost them both. Her mother had been a sweet, warm, comic, gorgeous companion who needed all Holly's love. Robert had needed little. Yet he had left her somebody to fill her heart.

Returning home after the swimming triumph, Holly told her excited stepdaughter to calm down and get her homework done.

'Oh, groan, must I?'

'Of course you must. I'll get supper and we can take it into the garden if you like.'

'OK. I'll do boring old homework. It's French. How I hate French.'

'For someone who hates it, I heard you singing a very long French song.'

'That's different. This is stupid verbs. But I've also got to write a poem for English. That'll be fun.'

Miranda took the stairs two at a time, and energetically slammed her bedroom door. Silence fell. Holly looked at her watch and saw she needn't get their picnic supper for half an hour. Sitting down, she sighed. She kept thinking about Paul Deslauriers. His elegant, tall figure, his French voice, echoed

21

in her thoughts. She wished he would go away. When she had refused that amazing invitation to stay in the South of France, he had actually looked shocked. It irritated her. Why should she and Miranda jump at the out-of-the-blue chance to go to Provence, for heaven's sake? Her grandparents had ignored Miranda for the entire nine years of her life, except for silly birthday cards. Now they apparently took it for granted that Holly and Miranda would be deeply grateful. They must jump to attention and cancel every arrangement. Holly and Miranda had their own lives. Thanks to Robert they were well provided for. They didn't need the St Martins, and up until now the St Martins certainly hadn't needed them.

And yet . . . Holly did not quite understand why the invitation made her cross. Did it mean that in her heart she thought she ought to have accepted?

Going to the french windows, she stared out at nothing in particular. A blackbird was hopping by. She was so still that it did not flutter, scolding, away. Then the telephone rang and bird and girl were both startled.

'Supposing it's him,' thought Holly.

It was.

'Madame – oh, I'm sorry, Holly. Do you think I might call round for a moment or two?'

'To try and persuade me, I suppose.'

'Well. Yes. Will you at least allow me to try?'

She could scarcely refuse and she rang off, groaning inwardly. But she didn't get the chance to worry for long; five minutes later the door bell rang.

'I telephoned from a box on the corner. I hope it's all right?' he said, seeing her surprise.

'Imagine coming all this way. You must have been sure I'd see you.'

'Well, I hoped,' he said, with a slight laugh.

They went into the sitting room and sat down and she offered him some sherry, but he refused. He wouldn't take her time, he said, he'd stayed too long yesterday. There were just a couple of things he felt he ought to say.

There was a rather curious pause. Holly waited, fixing her eyes seriously on him. He thought how young she looked. Vulnerable, young and very English.

He said, choosing his words carefully, 'Jacqueline and Christian have always very much regretted, you know, that they never had the chance to meet you and your stepdaughter. They were hurt. About Robert never going to see them. You don't believe that, do you?' he added speaking more quickly, as if afraid she was going to say something none too kind about his friends. He seemed determined to make her listen. Holly thought, 'But it won't do any good.'

'Of course I believe you if you say so. I'm sorry *they* are sorry. Perhaps we could go to see them some time. But not this summer. I'm afraid I sound a bit ungrateful.'

'It isn't a question of gratitude, madame. I mean, Holly.'

'You really find it hard to use first names straight away, don't you?'

She looked at him in a more friendly way, escaping the subject of the St Martins.

But he didn't answer that; did not let her get away from the reason he'd come.

'Family matters are so difficult. I've never talked

23

about Robert to Jacqueline, although we are close friends. I have never asked her what happened between them. Do *you* know?'

'Just that he didn't go to France. Of course, as I told you, his work took him all over the world.'

'Noticeably not to Provence. Except that once.'

'Yes, before he married Sally. Did you meet them then?'

'Quite a lot at the Rossignols. I always wondered why the visit wasn't repeated.'

Holly decided to be frank. In any case, she'd seen at their previous meeting that he hadn't much believed her excuses for Robert.

'So did I. When I first asked him, I'd only known him a few weeks, and he was vague. After we married, I wanted us all to go and see his parents. But he got out of it so often that it was obvious he had no intention of going. And then, somehow, afterwards I couldn't ask any more.'

'They quarrelled about something,' Paul said thoughtfully. 'Usually if families get bitter, it's over money.'

'Money!' exclaimed Holly with youthful scorn. 'That's not possible. Robert was a terrific success. And aren't the St Martins rather rich?'

He actually looked amused.

'Because people are wealthy doesn't mean they don't want more. On the contrary.'

There was a moment's silence. Holly reflected. And sighed.

'Anyway, neither of us knows what it was about. And it's in the past now. Over and forgotten.'

'But Jacqueline can't forget it. Which is why she wants to see her grandchild so much.'

'What's to stop her coming over here?' said Holly impatiently. The conversation was getting on her nerves again.

'She's very delicate and easily tired. Not really supposed to travel at all. I should imagine that's why she didn't come to visit Robert in London years ago. She and his father must have hoped he'd come to France again one day. And then . . . his death. It was a terrible shock. Much, much worse for you and his daughter, of course. But there is also something tragic in losing a son who is already lost to you.'

He saw that the words reached her.

'I'm certain she'd come to see you if she could,' he added. 'The St Martins aren't young. Christian is nearly seventy. They've never seen Robert's child. Isn't it natural that their thoughts should turn towards her?'

'Rather late in the day. She's nine.'

'I agree. But there it is. They long to see her.'

He sat opposite her, not sprawling as Mike Armstrong did, but straight back, elegantly composed. His dark eyes looked at her almost as if he could read her thoughts. She hoped he couldn't.

'So here I am, asking you to change your mind. Do come,' he said, gently persuasive.

Holly disliked being forced to refuse all over again. She looked out of the window at the syringa, frowning. Then turned and said in a rush, '*Please* don't ask me again. We simply can't come to France this summer to stay with them. We really can't. Our Kent holiday was fixed months ago and Miranda's so looking forward to it.'

'She'd look forward more to the Côte d'Azur.'

'No she wouldn't!' said Holly, stung. 'She doesn't

know her grandparents, she's never set eyes on them. I agree she ought to go eventually, but not now, not when our holiday's all fixed. And didn't you tell me they're giving this huge party? All those French people we've never met. It would be an ordeal for me, let alone a little girl of nine.'

Her usually pale cheeks turned pink, even her nose, the youngest thing in a young face, blushed with determination and annoyance.

There was a pause.

He suddenly said, 'You don't like them.'

'I never said so.'

'There are many ways of saying something without words. You haven't forgiven them for neglecting him. Are you quite fair? Didn't *he* neglect *them*?'

'I don't know. How can I? I'm prejudiced. But I'm not going to take her to Provence.'

'Why?'

'I told you. Our holiday. And that great party they're giving and the foreign atmosphere and –'

'Miranda is foreign, as you call it. She's half French.'

Holly wasn't being polite but she was rattled.

'Yes, Robert was French but she's never lived anywhere but England and doesn't think of herself as French. Neither do I. And she can't speak a word of French anyway.'

'Children learn quickly.'

That wasn't all he meant.

'I'm sorry,' said Holly flatly.

She was wearing an old, brown cotton dress with big patch pockets and round her neck was an amber necklace. She had been fiddling nervously with the silky beads. Now she plunged her hands into her pockets and Paul Deslauriers thought the hands were probably being made into fists. Her face was stormy.

'Have you asked your stepdaughter what she thinks? She might like the idea of Provence.'

Just then, to Holly's dismay, a voice shouted from upstairs, 'You know that poem I've got to write? I've done it. Shall I come and read it to you?'

'Have you done all the French verbs?' Holly shouted back, standing at the open door.

'Every boring one.'

Miranda appeared on the landing, said winningly, 'OK?' and slid down the banisters. Holly couldn't help laughing.

'There's a visitor. You'd better come and meet him.'

'Could the visitor hear the poem too?' said Miranda, never averse to an audience.

She marched into the sitting room. Paul stood up and shook her hand.

'I've heard a lot about you,' he said with what Holly thought a fine disregard for the truth.

'Have you?' said Miranda in her friendly way. 'Are you French?'

'Miranda –' from Holly in disapproval.

'Well, he is, isn't he?'

'Yes, I'm French,' said Paul. 'My name is Deslauriers.'

'I'm half French, you know, and my dad was quite French but he lived here in England. Can I read my poem?'

Holly said yes and Paul said it would be nice and they both sat down. Holly wondered if he was going to play fair. It would be very easy to start telling

Miranda about the South of France. She'd be fascinated – what child wouldn't? But he said nothing, leaning back in the manner of an attentive audience. Miranda took her place in the middle of the room.

'It's called *Gipsy's Song*. This is it.

> A wandering gipsy girl am I
> Once I was part of a fair,
> I organised the coconut shy
> And I left my life at that.
>
> But I used to like to lonely be
> I liked to be by myself,
> I didn't like to have company
> So I ran away one day.
>
> I built myself a little hut
> Near a sparkling stream
> I lived on root and berry and nut
> And anything I could scavenge.'

Silence. She looked expectantly from one to the other.

'It's very good,' said Paul. 'Just the sort of poem I like. And some of the lines don't rhyme, so it's what they call free verse.'

'I prefer it not all rhyming. I could have made them if I'd wanted to,' said Miranda carelessly.

'It's lovely, darling. But I didn't know you liked being by yourself so much.'

'Oh, Holly, it's a *poem*,' was the pitying reply. The front door bell rang three times and Miranda added eagerly, 'That's Claudia, can I go and watch telly next door? It's *Top of the Pops*.'

With a hasty goodbye, she skidded out.

There was the silence which falls when someone leaves the room.

'What a nice child,' he said.

'She reminds me of a grasshopper. Lots of hopping and singing,' said Holly, adding in her quick way, 'It was good of you not to tell her how marvellous France is, and paint a terrific picture to tempt her.'

He raised his eyebrows.

'I'd scarcely use persuasion on a child. The person I want to convince is you.'

'I suppose it is. Sorry.'

'No, you are not sorry, you're pleased to have made up your mind not to go. But there's something I'd like to ask. May I?'

She had lost her uncomfortable feelings. She said vaguely, 'Anything.' The problem was over now and she even smiled.

'Are you right to keep that child from her relations? Are you actually thinking about *her* at all? Or only of yourself?'

She was very taken aback. He spoke with his slightly formal French manner, but what he said was far more blunt than anything she had previously said to him. She was offended.

'You mean I'm being selfish.'

'Yes, I do.'

An uneasy, guilty, disturbed feeling which had never quite left her since his visit the day before came back in a rush. She said nothing for quite a long time. She did not look at him but stared at the floor, trying, trying to see what was right. She thought about Robert, not of the times he'd been cold and remote, but when he and she and Miranda had been

29

happy together, when Miranda had made him laugh. She thought of his deep love for Miranda's mother. Poor Sally, what a short life she had had. With an effort of imagination, Holly tried to think about those French grandparents. What had Paul said? They had 'lost a son already lost to them'.

She looked up at last.

He was sitting very still.

'Very well. We'll come.'

He didn't give a satisfied smile or become expansive as people do after they've won an argument. All he said was, 'But you don't want to.'

'Not a bit. How rude I sound.'

'But you're speaking the truth. I like it much more than the English habit of wrapping things up. I'm glad you've decided what you have, even though you don't like the idea. I can't help also thinking that you'll find yourself enjoying the Rossignols. People do,' he finished drily.

She was scarcely listening. She was still facing what she'd given up.

'We've been lent a little cottage in Kent. Quite near where my mother and I used to live. It faces the sea and at night you can hear the waves if you wake up. Miranda and I have been there before. We love the coast, we go swimming even when it's raining. What we like best is when the tide's out and there are such miles of sands, rock pools and crabs and all kinds of things to look at. English seaside things.'

'I'm afraid our sea has almost no tide. But maybe you'll enjoy swimming when it is very warm. People even swim at midnight.'

'Really?' she said absently, and then, 'You're right. I shouldn't stop her being with her family.'

They walked to the door as they'd done the previous evening. He took her hand in the same foreign way and kissed it.

'You're a gallant loser. I promise we'll do everything we can to make you happy.'

When he'd gone she went back to the sitting room and threw herself on the sofa. How horrid big decisions were. She hadn't made a single one since poor Robert was killed, except to decide that she and Miranda would go on living here. But this odd, attractive man who'd just left had brought with him from France not a present for Miranda, but something as ominous as the apple of discord in the myth. He'd reminded Holly that half of Miranda belonged to another nation. Holly loved her stepdaughter with the same protective almost fierce love she'd felt for her mother. She tried to imagine what it would be like at the House of Nightingales. There wasn't a single photograph of Robert's parents or their home among his papers. The only photographs he'd left had been of Sally on their honeymoon.

She would have to talk Miranda into liking the idea of giving up Kent and going to France. Why did she think that would be difficult, when she'd been afraid Paul Deslauriers would succeed only too well? 'Because he knows it and would make it sound magic,' thought Holly. 'But I don't know it. And however beautiful it is, I wish, I wish, we weren't going.'

31

2

Nice airport was crowded with suntanned people who all seemed to Holly to be rushing into each other's arms. The heat had struck both her and Miranda like a blow on the head as they came out of the plane, but inside the big echoing lounge was air-conditioned and cool. Miranda, hanging on to her hand, managed a sort of dance. She was pale with excitement.

Holly felt very conscious of just how untravelled she was. It was six years since her one trip abroad to Greece. She looked round anxiously, wondering what on earth she'd do if Paul wasn't there to meet them. 'I suppose I'll have to ring the hotel,' she thought. The idea of telephoning in French was appalling.

'Miranda, can you see him?'

'He's here!' cried Miranda in triumph. Paul came towards them through the crowds.

'Nice to see you both. How was the flight?'

'Terrific,' said Miranda, beaming. 'The air hostess gave me these. I may need them later, mayn't I?'

She exhibited a sticky handful of paper packets marked sugar, salt and pepper.

Paul agreed that they'd be most useful. He took the girls to a corner of the lounge where a large group of people surrounded a huge revolving turntable piled and scattered with luggage. People watched and snatched. Holly joined Miranda in trying to spot their suitcases. Ah, there they were. Holly had tied them with crimson labels.

Picking up the cases, Paul congratulated her. Somebody last month had arrived at the hotel and discovered that he'd taken the wrong case. It had been the twin of his own but, when he had opened it, it contained nothing but camping equipment, a folding tent and some tinned food.

Paul's car, a white open one, was in a car park shaded by palm trees. As they crossed the road to the car, the heat hit the girls again, their eyes were dazzled and Holly wished she'd brought Miranda's straw hat. Paul, seeing the child screwing up her eyes, said it would be cooler when they started to drive and there were lots of roads with trees. Holly was put in the front, Miranda in the back.

'I'd ask you to sit next to me, Miranda, but I'm afraid in France children aren't allowed in the front.'

'OK,' said Miranda philosophically. Now and then she leaned forward to shout remarks in Holly's ear.

As the journey began, Holly looked round curiously. It was a long time since her trip to Greece. She noticed the remarkable difference in the light. She and Miranda had left London on one of those dull summer days when the clouds are greyish, the colours a muted dull pearl, the air not exactly cold but chill. To find themselves here was like coming out of a dim house into a blazing garden. Along roads fringed with lofty palms were beds of brilliant orange and scarlet flowers thickly planted to make a

33

carpet of almost glaring colour. The many open cars driving by were full of people burned dark, shiny brown. The fields were honey coloured, the vineyards a vivid green, the mountains on the horizon a luminous purple and blue. It was this extraordinary light blue, sulphur yellow, purple, every shade of emerald, which painters discovered and after that forsook the rainy northern skies for ever.

Soon the trees shading the road were no longer palms but plane trees, their trunks freckled brownish and white, their branches lacing from one side of the road to the other. Holly looked round at Miranda, who was leaning back watching the arch of the trees. Apparently she was singing.

'You'll see Vanergues in a moment,' Paul said. He was driving down a curving road. They crossed an old hump-backed bridge and he pointed to a gap in the trees. There were vineyards in long lines converging into the distance, and beyond them scrubland of rocks and bushes, and beyond that again the land rose. On the top of a nearby hill was what looked like a town of toy bricks, a pile of blocks with a tiny bell-tower at its summit. Holly had seen hill villages before, during her Greek holiday. She'd never had the prospect of living in one. Vanergues had been built centuries before to defend its inhabitants against raiders – pirates from Italy. Even from far off, she could make out the walls which encircled it against enemies dead for hundreds of years.

The trees made a racing pattern of light and shade. Paul drove fast, and she knew her short time of freedom would soon be gone. She was dreading the prospect of her in-laws. She would have to put on a show and appear grateful to two people she'd never wanted to meet. Even Paul seemed a good friend compared with the two strangers waiting in that hill village up there.

They reached the sweep of road leading up to Vanergues. The ancient walls were stout and high. Parking on a sandy stretch under some trees, Paul swung their suitcases from the boot.

The village walls no longer formed a circle all round the village, there was a gap where a great gate had once stood. Through it, Holly saw a cobbled street lined with small shops. A picture gallery was next door to a fruiterer's, outside which were great mounds of peaches. A baker's on the opposite side sent a delicious aroma of fresh bread floating in the air. The walls then rose again, and cut into them was an entrance with the discreet sign, 'La Maison des Rossignols'.

'Here we are.'

He took them through a doorway. They crossed a broad terrace set about with tables. It was lunchtime and waiters were busy hurrying to and fro. People sat in the shade of beautiful old trees – it was like an Impressionist painting, Holly thought. Beyond them was a lichen-covered wall from which stretched the panorama of the country, all blue distances and vineyards and pure skies. To the left was a rambling old building. A cluster of doves on the roofs fluttered and settled.

'You must come and meet your grandparents, Miranda,' said Paul, capturing the little girl who had gone over to gape at the view. 'They're in a separate part of the house. They have a garden of their own.'

He took the girls into the hotel, down corridors and flights of steps, then through another door.

They came into what seemed to Holly a secret garden.

Olive trees threw their speckled shade on lawns, high walls were smothered with something like jasmine but with lavender-coloured flowers. The lawns were velvety, a fountain trickled in a bronze basin. There were white roses and pale geraniums. Completing the dreamlike picture, a woman in white lay stretched on a chaise longue. Seeing them, she put out a languid hand.

'*Enfin.*'

She spoke only French, and Holly, whose French was passable, answered a question or two about the journey, and introduced Miranda.

'Ah. The little one,' said the lady, and drew the child to her, kissing her three times. Miranda grinned as Jacqueline held her at arm's length.

'Charming. Charming. But she doesn't resemble her father.'

'I think she's rather like you,' said Paul.

Jacqueline St Martin gave a flattered little laugh. She began to talk to Holly, but all the time her eyes returned to Miranda, who'd wandered over to sit on the edge of the fountain.

Holly regarded her hostess with surprise amounting to wonder. When she knew she was coming to Vanergues, she'd tried to imagine Robert's mother. She'd wondered how she would feel to see in an older woman's face a reflection of her husband's lost image. It had never occurred to her that there would be nothing to see. How unexpected family likenesses were, sometimes so strong, sometimes totally lacking. Miranda didn't look like either of her parents – and Robert hadn't inherited a single resemblance to

36

his mother. She was as small as he had been tall, as plump as he had been thin. Her face was heart-shaped, her painted eyes blue, not brown. Her white hair, worn short, curled over her head. She had, thought Holly, a distinctly girlish air, her white dress was patterned with butterflies and she wore a good many gold bracelets which clinked as she moved. In curious contrast to her languid way of lying against a pile of cushions, her face was shrewd. The blue eyes probed.

'It's very interesting to meet you,' she said. 'My son never sent me a photograph of you. I wrote and asked him to. I recall that I wrote twice.'

Paul gave a slight laugh. 'Jacqueline has a long memory when she doesn't get something she wants.'

She pouted. 'I suppose I am a little spoiled but . . . when one's health is not strong.' She gave Paul a speaking look. 'My poor son was so bad at writing letters, so brilliant at writing books. He inherited my imagination, you know. A certain – what would one call it? – fantasy. And now,' with a brisk change of tone, 'here's my grandchild at last.' She dragged her eyes away from Miranda and, as she looked at Holly, used the curious French phrase, 'You do me great service.'

'We're glad to be here, aren't we, Miranda?' Holly said, translating back into English.

'Of course, but I say, Holly, I'm absolutely starving.'

'You must have some lunch,' said Paul, neatly rescuing Holly. 'I'm sure all you had on the plane was a sandwich. I'll order something.'

He disappeared through the doorway into the hotel. Jacqueline St Martin pointed to a chair and requested Holly to bring it nearer to her. Miranda leaned across the fountain basin and put her finger into the mouth of the bronze fish to stop it flowing. Then she removed her hand, and grinned to see the water burst out again.

Holly, meanwhile, was attacked by a barrage of questions. Her hostess was unashamedly curious. She asked about Sally: had she been a well-known journalist? had she earned a good deal of money? She enquired about her son's book sales, about the Richmond house, and if Holly had domestic help. Where had Holly met Robert? How long had they known each other before they married? How old had Holly been then? And now? Returning to the subject of the marriage, about which she appeared to know nothing, she asked which church they had been married in, and whether Holly had worn white?

Holly did not enjoy any of this. She was overwhelmed by the stream of questions, by the demand for an instant intimacy as if, because she was a daughter-in-law, she *must* reply to anything and everything. It was like being in a witness box. She answered politely but with caution. She found herself describing a perfectly happy marriage, a husband who was everything a young girl could wish. Jacqueline showed no signs of disbelief at this overrosy picture of the past. Perhaps she thought it natural for any young woman married to a St Martin. But she did ask why Robert hadn't taken Holly abroad with him. Holly said it had been because of Miranda's school. She'd stayed at home to look after her. Jacqueline fortunately didn't raise the point that it would have been easy for him to take them on working journeys which coincided with school holidays. Holly spoke of how hard Robert had worked, and how enormously successful his books still were.

'Of course, of course,' said Jacqueline St Martin, taking the compliment personally. 'And we've read them many times, my husband and I. They're translated into French. And into six other languages, you know.'

Holly did.

'We went to Nice to see the film they made of *The Summer's Danger*. People were queuing,' said Jacqueline.

Holly nodded. She didn't say how much Robert had complained about the film. He'd said the plot had been bungled and that the acting was thin. He'd been gloomy about the film for months after its London premiere.

'Now I must take your visitors away for a while, my dear,' said Paul, reappearing. 'They scarcely ate on the plane. I've arranged something for them.'

Jacqueline gave a little scream. 'Nothing to eat! No wonder my grandchild is as thin as a piece of grass.'

Paul took the girls back to the terrace which was now more crowded still. Many of the people having lunch turned to look at them, and almost everybody seemed to know Paul. One pretty, dark woman held out her hand to be kissed.

He didn't stay with Holly and Miranda during their delicious meal, but came to fetch them afterwards to take them up to their room.

'I thought you might like a siesta. It must seem very hot to you after England,' he said, pulling the curtains of the room. 'Most people like to sleep for a while in the afternoon. Especially after a journey.'

Miranda made a martyred grimace, but Holly thanked him. He said if they'd come down to the private garden at five, Christian St Martin would be home by then.

At the door he turned and said teasingly, 'Poor Holly. A very social day.'

'We're having a lovely time.'

'Mm,' he said in a disbelieving voice.

When he had gone, Miranda jumped up on to her bed and bounced.

'What a room. Have you *seen* the bathroom? It's huge! And two balconies. And there are chairs and a table on one, do you think we could have breakfast out there? Isn't it smashing? Claudia would be pea-green if she saw me.'

Bouncing harder, she flew into the air. Then she climbed down to look at the door of the wardrobe, painted with birds. 'Do you think they're doves?' Miranda made a tour of the room, examining everything as closely as a detective. The bathroom was very splendid, with turquoise tiles patterned with water-lilies, a thick white carpet and gold dolphin heads for taps. Huge, fluffy towels were embroidered simply: 'Rossignols'.

Miranda, fascinated by everything, declared she wasn't tired, who could possibly be tired in the afternoon? Slumping down on her large bed, she fell asleep.

Holly watched the little olive-tinted face. Awake, she was never still. Asleep, she was a mouse. Striped hair, fair and dark, lay in a fan on the pillow. Holly had taken off the little girl's dress, indeed it was very hot, and Miranda lay in brief blue pants and that was all. 'How small she is,' thought Holly. 'How I love her.'

As she, too, drifted into sleep, she tried to banish from her mind a possessive look which she'd seen in Jacqueline St Martin's face when looking at Miranda. It had only been for a moment, but it was unmistakable. It had scared her.

Miranda settled down well during the following days. She went exploring, disappeared down unexpected flights of stairs and through staff doors, appearing like a jack-in-the-box in the kitchens. She made friends with the chef, the hall porters and the girl who brought their breakfast.

Holly herself didn't feel as out-of-place as she'd imagined. The Rossignols was certainly beautiful. One evening Paul invited her for a drink on the terrace, and talked about the old house. The House of Nightingales was, in parts, over six hundred years old. In the Middle Ages and until the French Revolution it had been a convent dedicated to a local saint, Réparate, who'd been martyred by the Romans in Provence. In statues she was sometimes shown with a nightingale on her wrist. The legend said that she'd loved wild birds, and the nightingales had come in flocks to the convent grounds, to sing in chorus all day long. From the distant past the building had been known locally as Les Rossignols.

Here and there were traces of the old convent, a pointed arch, a faded wall-painting of the Virgin and Child and, in a corridor near the kitchen, a painting of the saint with a bird on her wrist.

After the nuns were driven out, the Rossignols became a posting inn for travellers on their way through the mountains to Italy. Later it was turned into a farm. During the Great War the district became very poor and an artist wounded on the Somme – his name was Alain Tessier – returned to his native land and bought the crumbling old farm. He had lived here, painting landscapes, ruined castles, Roman theatres, jetties, fields of rosemary. There were some of his Provençal paintings in the dining room.

'Tessier is much admired now. Never when he lived, which is often the case with painters, unfortunately,' Paul said. 'He was a romantic. He planted the gardens with bushes, to tempt back the nightingales to sing to him all day.'

'Poor man. Surely he knew they only sing at night?'

'That's in England, Holly,' said Paul, smiling. 'We often hear them in daytime. I've seen one perched on a branch. But not, I'm afraid, in our gardens. You'll like Tessier's paintings. He was a kind of poet in paint. Why is it we French paint so well, but it's you British who write the best poetry? I don't expect you to answer that. I'll finish the history of the Rossignols.'

When Tessier had died, Christian St Martin had come along. He was young and full of ideas, had always wanted a hotel, and invested every franc in the place. It was in the late 1930s, and the South of France was changing; it was no longer the place where rich aristocrats came only in winter. Young Americans – Scott Fitzgerald, Hemingway – came to spend summers in Provence. Picasso visited Antibes, and had dinner at the Rossignols.

Over the years the hotel grew steadily more famous. People liked the odd-shaped, ancient buildings, the stone floors, the atmosphere and, most of all, the cooking. There was a talented chef. Christian built an outdoor swimming pool, and a ceramic artist from the potters' town of Vallauris designed tiles for it.

'Sunflowers and lizards and morning glories,' said Holly. 'I've seen them. Beautiful.'

She enjoyed all Paul had told her. Later that evening she went to find the wall-paintings. There they were, so faded they seemed to be vanishing into the past. Sweet, sad echoes of very long ago.

After that evening when they talked for nearly an hour, Holly didn't see much of Paul. He smiled at her at a distance across the terrace, or came to have a word, but the hotel was full and she knew how busy he was. She never saw anybody among the hotel staff – the housekeepers and chambermaids, the elderly, gnomelike François at reception and the pretty, plump girl who took his place when he was off duty, the troop of young men and girls in the big kitchens – who wasn't busy from morning until night. Paul did take her one morning with Miranda to the kitchens and introduced them to Jean Du Loup, the celebrated chef. He was swarthy, forty-five, with a mobile, haggard face on which toughness and impatience were very clear. He accepted Holly's compliments about the food (which was indeed wonderful) like an actor after a huge success.

Holly and Miranda had been given a bedroom in the public part of the hotel. That was a relief to Holly, who wouldn't have enjoyed living in

Jacqueline's private domain. And seeing the other guests was fun. Often when they came downstairs after a balcony breakfast, Holly and Miranda would recognise some famous face. The first time this happened Miranda said in her high, clear voice, 'Look, Holly! There's the man in the telly serial.' On another morning (jogged by Holly to speak quietly) she hissed, '*That's* the girl in the space film. The one who was friends with the robot.'

It was ironic, thought Holly, to remember that she had worried about bringing her stepdaughter into this unfamiliar French-speaking world. Miranda took to it like a duck to water. Jacqueline cultivated young married friends with children. 'It's strange how they like me,' she said to Holly with a self-satisfied smile. She seemed to expect a compliment, an eager, 'But *of course* they do!'

Holly merely smiled in reply and said nothing. She didn't want to pay compliments to a lady who paid them to herself. But, through the young marrieds, Miranda soon met half a dozen children of about her own age. Wearing skimpy bikinis, they sported in the Rossignols pool like dolphins. They sat on the grass playing mysterious games. At night, at their own table in the restaurant, the group of children had grown-up supper. Miranda was soon an accepted friend of them all.

What astounded Holly was Miranda's French. It was the subject she liked least at school: she never managed an entire sentence without help and her accent was vile. All this suddenly changed. She began to speak real French with a pretty accent, to exchange remarks with her new friends and laugh at their jokes. Holly heard her talking French as if she'd lived here for months.

The little girl was also a good deal with her grandmother. Jacqueline developed the habit of sending for the child, rather too often, to sit with her in the garden. Jacqueline never (as Miranda remarked to Holly) went for a walk, so Miranda had to sit by the chaise longue and chat. Sometimes if Holly happened to be there, she saw a look of boredom in Miranda's eyes; she was a restless soul. But she was polite and good-natured, and Jacqueline was quick to offer temptations. Fresh blackcurrant juice for elevenses, mouth-watering biscuits made by Jean Du Loup, wonderful home-made ice creams and big, expensive French books for children, possibly Robert's, over which one young head, striped fair and dark, and one elderly curly white one would bend, with occasional giggles from Miranda and looks of triumph from Jacqueline.

Holly far preferred it when Miranda was with her friends, with the twins Charles and Yves, whose father, said Miranda, 'has this gynormous motor boat. He makes boats, you know. Half the ones in the harbour comes from his boat-building place.' There were other boys and girls, including Sophie, the leader and the eldest, with waist-length fair hair. She was a good swimmer, but Miranda boastfully reported to Holly that she'd beaten her in a race. Best of all there was Pierrette, plump, dark and friendly, with a fringe touching her eyes. She was exactly the same age as Miranda, and the two children soon became inseparable.

Certainly Miranda was having a wonderful holiday. Holly wished that *she* was. It was ungrateful not to appreciate the sunshine, the blue and honey-

45

coloured countryside, the scent of flowers, the luxury, the exquisite meals. But Jacqueline's grabbing way with Miranda upset her. 'Am I jealous?' thought Holly. Yet it would have been easy to share with another kind of woman. Something in Jacqueline disturbed her. At times that first feeling of being almost afraid returned to Holly in a wave. She told herself she was being ridiculous. She still felt it.

She now saw something of her father-in-law, Christian St Martin, and scarcely liked him better than Jacqueline. He did look like Robert: he was tall, heavily built, with Robert's eyes and supercilious smile. He spent much of his time in his hotel office, but often sat in the garden with his wife. Holly had hoped to like him, for Paul spoke of him affectionately. But although she tried hard, she couldn't. Slow-speaking, solemn, he had been handsome when young, and his heavy looks still had a sort of nobility, like those of a statesman in the last century. He was very polite, standing up when Holly came into the gardens, shaking hands to bid her good morning, raising the panama hat he wore in the sun if he saw her in the distance. But it was only too obvious what he thought about women. He had a kind of patronising kindness when he spoke to Holly, a way of absently nodding if she talked. The expression in his eyes showed that he was certain she would never say anything of interest. Holly thought he didn't pay all that much attention to Jacqueline when she spoke either, and she knew it. There was a gleam of annoyance in her blue eyes sometimes.

When Paul opened his mouth, Christian's expression altered. A man was talking.

'I suppose I should be amused at such an archaic

way of going on,' thought Holly. 'He's a leftover; he behaves like Edwardian men must have done. Women only rate to be provided with extra cushions for their chaises longues. Goodness, how can Jacqueline bear it?'

Very well, it seemed, apart from the gleams. Jacqueline was vivacious with her husband, she was talkative, demanding, imperious and spoiled.

From the first day they met, Holly wasn't drawn to her. She had been made uncomfortable by her intense curiosity. Her mother-in-law gave Holly the distinct impression that a cold selfishness was hidden under the diamonds and smiles. And why the chaise longue? She didn't look ill. At times she positively glowed with energy, lying against the cushions. Worst of all was the possessiveness with Miranda, which seemed to be growing day by day.

It was true that Holly had half expected something like that, even before she'd left England. She made up her mind that, however much fuss the grandparents made of Miranda, she would understand and not resent it. Miranda was such an engaging creature, the elderly couple would be sure to spoil her. But, although she'd told herself all this, Holly was still disturbed.

And she missed Miranda's sparkling company. In this hotel filled with people, in this magical place, Holly was lonely.

One afternoon when Jacqueline was having her three-hour siesta and Miranda had gone to spend the day with Charles and Yves on their boat, Holly went into the private garden. She sat, her book forgotten, staring at the fountain's thin spray and listening to the soporific cooing of the doves on the roof. She remembered the little saint and her nightingales . . . glancing up, there was Paul.

'I didn't hear you.'

'You were miles away. Hello, Holly. Days since I've talked to you.' He stood looking down at her, raising his eyebrows with a quizzical, 'How goes it?'

'Fine.'

'Are you enjoying the Rossignols? Have you everything you want?'

'Now, Paul, of course we have!'

He sat on the grass near her, and said, leaning back and looking at her, 'I'm not asking about Miranda whom I keep seeing with that gang of children. I'm asking about you. I feel a bit respons-ible for you – I did more or less drag you here.'

'The Rossignols is lovely. I'm grateful.'

'I'm not sure I quite believe you. You're not like Miranda, who spends the entire day in the pool. She'll turn into a frog. What have *you* been doing with yourself?'

'Shopping in the village now and then. Swimming, though not as often as Miranda. Oh, yes, and I did notice a bus in the square. It had Juan les Pins on it. I thought I might take it one afternoon, and see a bit more of Provence.'

He looked shocked.

'Of course you must! You've practically been a prisoner; it's all my fault. I get so wrapped up in the job and – how many days is it since you came? Poor Holly, how bored you must have been.'

'Bored! I only meant –'

'Don't be English and start apologising because I'm in the wrong,' he said, laughing. 'Have dinner with me tonight. I don't mean here. Somewhere away from Vanergues.'

'I'd love to.'

'Good, then that's settled.'

But he still looked at her with concern, and Holly was touched.

Miranda returned from her day on the boat in high spirits, changed into a best dress and left for what she told Holly was 'Summer Guy Fawkes'. It seemed that every summer there was a big international firework display at Cannes. This year there were six countries in competition, and tonight it would be the Japanese. According to Miranda, an instant expert, they were going to win. The fireworks, enormous, dramatic and very beautiful, were set off to burst in the sky over the sea.

When Miranda had gone, Holly had an hour of solitude to get ready for her own date. She had a bath and dressed slowly, deciding on a dress she'd bought in Richmond before they left for France but had not yet worn. It was in southern colours, coffee and flame, with a halter neck which left her shoulders bare. Looking at herself in the long glass, she thought she needed a bracelet, and fastened on one of Miranda's made of small brown beads. She and Miranda often swapped things, and tonight Miranda was wearing Holly's watch.

Down on the terrace the dusk was falling, it was dim and bluish and the view had turned into a milky mist pricked with faraway lights. A hand touched her arm. It was Paul, looking handsome in a white jacket.

'*Que vous êtes belle*. Very beautiful.'

'Oh good,' she thought. 'And you look lovely, too. Why can't one say it? Some women would.'

49

It was almost dark as they drove from Vanergues down the winding road they'd taken on the day she and Miranda had arrived. There was the stone bridge. Now they were under the long archway of plane trees.

'We're going to the sea. To watch the waves while we have our dinner.'

'It sounds gorgeous.'

'Don't expect too much, Holly. Suppose the food's disappointing?'

'You'd never choose a restaurant where that happened.'

'What confidence you have in me. Thank you. But it's probably true. Who can enjoy an evening when the cooking is bad?'

He drove on down tree-edged roads.

'Paul,' she suddenly remarked.

'Holly?'

'About what you said just now. I don't agree at all. I'm sure one can be blissful during a revolting meal, and miserable eating a feast.'

'Holly, Holly, I'm very sorry to discover that the English still talk romantic nonsense.'

They had left the country now and were driving into the outskirts of a town, crossing a busy auto-route junction and finally coming to Juan les Pins. Holly thought it had a sedate, Victorian look. There were palm-filled squares with well-kept gardens, and old hotels with painted grey shutters and marble steps. On many corners were the sort of cafés one saw in old paintings of Paris, with broad windows and a glimpse of gilded mirrors behind polished mahogany bars. The shops, too, were elegant. At the end of a broad boulevard was the marble statue of a girl in flowing robes. She was like the figures which decorate last-century opera houses.

'Juan les Pins hasn't changed much for a hundred years, has it, Paul?'

'Ah. Wait until we get to the promenade.'

He turned the car at a corner to a broad road running by the sea. Here every old house and garden had vanished. In their place rose block after block of large white flats with balconies and awnings. All the blocks had ecstatic names over their entrances. 'Vista of Beauty', 'Eden Paradiso', 'Mimosa Mirage', 'California Arcady'.

'In winter there's scarcely a soul in them,' said Paul. 'I know a writer who comes down every year in November, and stays here, working away, until the middle of May. He lives in one of the largest blocks for almost nothing. When the holidaymakers arrive, back he goes to his family outside Paris. His parents kindly keep his room for him. He said the holiday-makers are like migratory birds. They land in enormous noisy flocks and, just before October, off they go.'

'Which season do *you* prefer? When they're all here, or when they've gone?'

'Oh, I like the noise and the pace. Yet there's something rather pleasant and melancholy about the winter beaches. You see, Holly, I'm easy.'

Parking the car under some trees, they crossed to the promenade. A restaurant was built about ten feet higher than the shelving beach, with steps leading to the shore. The restaurant, Chez les Pêcheurs, was nautical, with windows like portholes and a sign showing a green fish in lights.

The maître d'hôtel greeted them warmly, he knew

51

Paul well, and they were given one of the best tables, by a window overlooking the beach and the black void which was the sea. Holly asked Paul to choose the meal. While he ordered, she sat watching a long white line, which must be the breaking waves

He put down the menu and looked at her. 'What are you thinking?'

'About Miranda. Do you know, she's never swum in the Mediterranean.'

'I'll bring you both down here.'

'*Would* you?'

'I'd be glad to. Early one morning.

'She's so responsive,' he thought. 'How young she looks, eagerly smiling. Yet she is a widow and life must have marked her in some way.'

During the meal she asked him about the other two St Martin hotels, in Germany and Spain. One was an old Bavarian coaching inn by a river, he said. The Spanish one had been a private house – they'd even kept the ballroom and a harp which had belonged to the owner's daughter.

'Christian and I have lots of plans . . . We argue over those, as you can imagine.'

'How long have you worked for the St Martins?'

'Well, I – that is, would you think it conceited if I said I don't exactly work *for* them. Actually, I own part of the hotels.'

She couldn't help smiling.

'I see you're laughing at me. You're right. My stupid masculine vanity made me tell you that.'

'I was smiling with surprise. I was impressed. It's terrific. The St Martins must lean on you rather a lot – I mean, Monsieur isn't young and it's a big job.'

'I wish he'd lean more.'

'Doesn't he?'

'Holly, it would be a miracle if we agreed about a lot of things. A man nearing seventy and one of thirty. Forty years between us – a lifetime. He's a magnificent hotelier but he has his prejudices, some of them almost unshiftable. I don't know why I'm telling you all this.'

'Why not? I'd tell you things.'

His expression changed slightly. 'There must be things you wouldn't tell me.'

She wondered if he meant about her marriage. And then it came into her mind that he guessed she was worried by Jacqueline monopolising Miranda, but would never complain to *him* about it. She was sure he noticed everything at the Rossignols. The place had been created by Christian, but Holly thought Paul's was the hand which ruled it now, making it the place it was. And it was because he knew what was happening to her that he'd come to find her in the garden.

She didn't mind the fact that he was dining with her only out of kindness, and because he still felt responsible for having brought her to France. She liked him feeling guilty about her. She liked him very much. She enjoyed his company, the way he looked; his voice fascinated her. It was expressive and deep, its accent amused her, and he seemed to mean more than the words he used. His English was faultless, but his thoughts seemed to her very French. They were different, unexpected. His manner, too. He seemed to understand her, and she felt natural and free with him, as if she could talk about anything and everything. Except about Jacqueline grabbing at Miranda, for that might hurt or worry him.

They talked of his days at university in Aix-en-Provence and then about Holly's life with her mother in Kent. About cold winters and walks on deserted freezing beaches at Christmas. He told her he'd worked in London after leaving university, and they spent quite a time trying to discover if, in some coincidental way, they'd actually been in the same place at the same time. At a theatre? A concert? St Paul's? The Abbey?

'You're too young to have been anywhere but at school or walking on your beloved beaches,' he said.

The restaurant began to empty, the candles had burned down. They said goodbye to the maître d'hôtel, and crossed the empty road. There was dew on the car seats, and he took off his jacket for her to sit on. She protested.

'If you don't do as I ask, I shall drive home without you.'

'Paul, what a mean advantage.'

'I always take those when there's the chance.'

They drove home in friendly silence. The moon wasn't white but the colour of an apricot. She saw a mass of fireflies under some trees. The hotel terrace was deserted and silent, the doves had flown. A wave of scent drifted towards them.

'What a wonderful smell, what is it?'

'From a tree under the wall. Come and look.'

At the end of the terrace, growing up almost to touch the wall, was a tree covered with huge, creamy flowers, their scent so strong that Holly felt she was swimming in it.

'What a *strange* country you live in!' she said, turning to look at him. He pulled her close and began to kiss her. He put his hands on either side of her face and shut his eyes, and when he stopped the embrace and Holly opened her eyes, she saw him looking gravely down at her. They both smiled faintly then. She felt as if her heart would burst. They kissed again and the space between them melted; she let herself go, pressed against him, conscious of his mouth and his body and his strength. The heady scent bathed them from head to foot.

When they were apart he said slowly, '*Belle Anglaise*. You're lovely.'

'So are you.'

He shook his head and took her arm to walk with her into the hotel. At the foot of the stairs, away from the dozing night porter, he bent to kiss her hand. 'Thank you for being with me.'

She lingered.

'Now you must go, Holly.'

'Why?'

'Because I don't want you to.'

Up in her room she was awake for a long time. Miranda was breathing steadily and deeply; the hotel itself was asleep. But Holly lay thinking about Paul. To be so happy frightened her. Somebody said that falling in love was like surf riding. The waves were enormous and if you fell, you could break your neck.

'Holly, Holly,' said Miranda, as the sun poured into the room, 'breakfast is here and do wake up because the *pain chocolat* has to be eaten at once, so *Grand-mère* says.'

Holly dragged herself from sleep. A figure was sitting at the end of her bed. The maid had already put the tray on the balcony, and Miranda then went out and took the cover off a silver dish.

'Melted chocolate. *Imagines toi*.'

'Miranda,' yawned Holly, tying the belt of her cotton dressing-gown, 'are we going to have pidgin English all day?'

'I expect so.'

Holly came out into the sun to join her.

'*Grandmère*,' continued Miranda, attacking a croissant filled with chocolate, 'says I have a big talent for languages. She's taking me to Cap Trois Mille this morning. It's the hugest place all made of shops, you know, modern and sticking out into the sea, and she's going to buy me a sun dress. *Très chic*, she says.'

Holly was very surprised. Since when had Jacqueline gone anywhere?

'Are you sure, Miranda? I can't imagine your grandmother wanting to go out, let alone now it seems to be hotter each day.'

'Oh, she'll be OK,' said Miranda, never impressed with Jacqueline's delicate health. 'When *Grandpère* said she'd be tired she said "pooh". Besides, shopping's her thing and she likes Cap Trois Mille. We're leaving at quarter to nine, which is why I'm eating fast.'

Punctually at quarter to nine, Miranda, crisp and fresh with hair slicked down, hurried away.

Holly bathed and dressed, thinking all the time about Paul. She supposed it was naive to be so affected by kissing him last night. Most girls would take it as the usual end to a pleasant evening. She couldn't. Something deep and important, exciting, almost desperate, had happened in her heart.

56

When she went downstairs she was tense at the thought of seeing him. There was nobody on the terrace but a boy watering the flowers. The air smelled, not of night lilies, but wet earth. Disappointed, she went out into the village for a walk.

The walls of Vanergues, built against marauders centuries before, were so high that it was like walking in a small ravine. The huge stones sprouted with ferns. Turning a corner, she saw the open windows of a pottery, and a girl sitting working there. She looked at Holly and said good morning.

'Would you like to look round?' asked the girl, gesturing to the inside of the shop.

It was a kind of studio lined with shelves filled with pottery. There were vases, box ˙, teapots, scent bottles, every kind of plate. The colours were soft blue, greyish, lavender and a dove-brown, and the pottery was painted with figures. Girls, cats, men in tall hats, churches, mimosa trees. Picking up a decorated plate, Holly gave an exclamation. Across it danced an elf carrying a mushroom umbrella. The figure was uncannily like Miranda.

'I painted that yesterday, I'm afraid it isn't fired yet,' said the girl. She was dark and very Provençal, with cloudy black hair.

'It's so pretty. And very like someone in my family.'

'But of course. I saw your stepdaughter in the square.'

'So it *is* Miranda!'

'Everyone in the village knows about the grandchild. It was easy to guess who she was, and she reminded me of an imp. I'm glad you think it's like her.'

Holly looked at the angular dancing figure.

'Could I buy it?'

'I'd be delighted. It will be fired later this week. I'll keep it for you.'

'Céline?' said a man's quiet voice. Holly's nerves seemed to jump. Paul smiled at seeing her, then spoke to Céline about some new lamps for the hotel. They discussed the size and colour. When they'd finished, he said, 'Are you walking back, Holly?'

Strolling home he talked about Céline Cesar who had come to work in Vanergues a year before.

'Provence is the land of potters, as you probably know. Vallauris, for instance, where Picasso used to work, is a town of nothing else. More than a hundred potters. But Céline is so original. She suits Vanergues. By the way, how do you feel about getting up at seven tomorrow morning?'

'To swim? We'll be up at five if you like!'

'You really mean that? But seven will be fine and we'll breakfast on the beach.'

Miranda, very keen, declared later that it was dead easy to wake early. But after a day of shopping with her grandmother and swimming in the pool she slept as if stunned. Holly, too, was lulled by the long, sunny day, but nervous expectation woke her at half-past six.

She pulled the curtains to look out. The garden was very still, an almost unearthly silence brooded. The sky was lemon yellow slowing turning to crimson.

She woke Miranda who looked hazy, blinked, then remembered and leaped out of bed. They pulled sundresses over bikinis, collected towels; as the

58

village clock chimed seven, there was a tap at the door.

Paul, in T-shirt and jeans.

The roads were almost empty and when they reached the beach at Juan it was deserted except for one bronzed young man raking the sand.

'This is where I swim whenever I can get away,' Paul said. 'Guy owns the bar, he's an old friend. He'll give us breakfast. Well? Are we ready?'

The girls pulled off their sundresses, Paul his shirt and jeans. In trunks, Holly saw he was almost as dark brown as the boy raking the beach. His shoulders were very broad, his thin figure a triangle from shoulder to waist, graceful and strong.

The water was palish silver blue, the waves small, scarcely breaking. As they waded into the sea, Miranda shouted, 'Fish! Fish!' A shoal of wriggling things, fine as threads darted away.

The trio began to swim towards a raft. How blissful the water was. Holly dived down, came to the surface to see the misty shape of a white yacht on the horizon. Miranda called to Paul, 'Race you to the raft!'

They climbed up on to the raft, lay in the sun, dived, climbed up again. At last Paul said it was time for breakfast.

'I can see Guy opening the shutters. Who would like some fresh croissants?'

'I'm so hungry, I'm too weak to swim,' said Miranda.

'Which means I must lifesave you, I suppose?'

He swam obligingly back with Miranda hanging, limpetlike, to his shoulders.

Guy was waiting to welcome them, laying tables,

59

brewing coffee. He was fat and fiftyish, wearing only a pair of blue shorts, his sunburned chest covered with grey curls. He shook hands with the girls, and disappeared busily to the kitchen at the back of the bar.

Everybody was hungry, and the croissant-basket was refilled twice. The sun grew warmer. Their wet swimsuits dried as they drank their coffee and watched the sea. Taking a final croissant in a salty hand, Miranda went down to wander ankle deep in the waves.

'She swims well,' Paul said.

'She's proud of that.'

'She's enjoying France. She's happy,' he said, his eyes still on the shrimplike figure on the edge of the sea.

'She's always happy. Has been since we first met. Well, almost since then.'

'Was that soon after her mother died?'

'Six months. My mother had died too, and I had only known Robert a short while. He took me to see Miranda. She was rather a waif then, too thin and quiet. She was like –' Holly paused, looking for the words – 'like a flower which needed water. After Robert and I married and I was there all the time, she sort of bloomed.'

'*You* watered the flower.'

'Thank you for the compliment, but anyone fond of her could have done the trick, I imagine. Children like to feel safe. She's an affectionate little love.'

Holly wasn't looking at him, and didn't catch the fixed, almost intent expression his his eyes. She said, 'I must go and fetch her or she'll start swimming again. Then she'll drip all over your car on the way back.'

After their morning on the beach, Holly very much wanted to see him again not in the distance or in the St Martins' garden, but alone. He was always charming to her when they met with other people, and she saw, or thought she did, a look of caring for her in his face, and heard it in his voice. But seeing him in public at the Rossignols was a kind of half-excited disappointment. He did not ask her out again. The loneliness she'd felt on the afternoon he had come to find her returned, sharper than before.

Jacqueline was growing more possessive and doting over Miranda every day. The collection of the little girl's bikinis had now grown to six, Miranda had a drawer full of expensive sundresses, and the latest addition was two pairs of hand-made Italian sandals. Her grandmother was always sending for her, and although Miranda threw up her big eyes in a 'not again!' glance, she went padding off quite cheerfully. She certainly wasn't spoiled. She was too busy, too interested in the whole of this southern world, from a lizard to a flower.

'*Imagines toi*, Holly, *Grandmère* doesn't know the name of any flowers. I told her you know every single one at home.'

One morning, with Miranda gone once more to Cap Trois Mille to shop with her grandmother, Holly was on the terrace when Paul came looking for her. He was alone, and her heart jumped.

'Will you have some coffee with me, Holly? Come up to my office. You haven't seen it, have you?'

She was so happy that she had wings on her heels. They went upstairs to a spacious room on the first

61

floor. Windows overlooked the gardens; she caught a far glimpse of mountains. He pulled a chair to the open windows.

'There's always a slight breath of wind from the Alps, even when it's hottest,' he said. 'And today's going to be very hot.'

When coffee arrived and he handed her a cup, she met his eyes and smiled. He did not smile back.

For the first time she noticed that his handsome face looked strained. The strong light pouring in lit him harshly as if by arc lamps, and she saw the lines on his forehead and etched round his mouth. He didn't look himself, and she had an inexplicable return of alarm.

'Where's Miranda this morning?' was all he said.

'With her grandmother. Shopping again, I fear,' said Holly, deliberately casual.

'They get on well, don't they?'

The alarm – it had been absurd, hadn't it? – ebbed away.

'Isn't her French extraordinary, Paul? It seems almost a miracle to hear her talking, when I remember she couldn't speak a word at home.'

'Yes. She's very quick. She learns fast.'

She sipped her coffee. His voice was as strained as his face. It was odd. Why? He must be tired, she thought. Running the hotel was a responsibility, and Christian was getting old, and more weight must come heavily on Paul. Perhaps there was some trouble, even financial trouble, although this seemed so rich a world.

'There's something I must say to you, Holly.'

She looked up. She caught his tenseness and felt herself stiffen.

'Yes? What is it?'

'Jacqueline asked me to speak to you. She doesn't feel well enough to explain, and thought it better if I did. She and Christian want Miranda to remain with them in France.'

3

'What do you mean? Of course she can't remain, we have to be back at the beginning of September. School term starts.'

'You don't understand. They want to keep her.'

'*To keep her?*'

'To live here with them as their son's child. As a member of the family. They want her to make her home with them in France.'

'But that's impossible.'

'No, Holly. It isn't.'

The colour faded from her face. It was almost grey.

'Let me get this right. The St Martins have talked to you. And asked you to tell me they want Miranda. They want to steal her from me.'

'A rather melodramatic way of putting it.'

His strained voice was quiet. It made what he was saying the more terrible. She burst out, 'Melodramatic? It *is* melodramatic. You – you come over to England and invite Miranda and me to their party. You know I didn't want to come. We have our own life, we aren't dependent on these people –' the words rushed out like a flood. 'Now you ask me into your office and coolly tell me they intend to steal my stepdaughter. Steal her! What sort of people are they, for God's sake? How *dare* they think they can get away with it. And how dare they get *you* to do their dirty work.'

His face was set, he looked a stranger. She thought, 'I hope you know how I despise you for agreeing to tell me. Now I understand why I didn't want to come here. They were setting a trap for us.'

'Try to understand how they feel,' he said in his quiet, grave voice. 'Please be calm and at least try. Christian and Jacqueline aren't young any more. They have no family at all, not a soul. Not even distant relations. Their only son was estranged to them, we don't know why. Now he's dead. They have nobody.'

'And want to steal Miranda.'

'That word. How can you use it? After all, she's of their blood. Not yours.'

'I knew you'd throw that at me.'

She shuddered.

'When her grandparents die,' he continued in a reasonable way, 'the child will inherit part of an important business. The three St Martin hotels make a good deal of money. By then there may be a fourth.'

'She doesn't need money. She has her father's.'

'Scarcely the kind of fortune I'm talking about. Books like your husband's are not the great classics. They do not last.'

She looked down, pleating her skirt nervously until it was a mass of creases. Then suddenly looked up.

'Robert's royalties aren't small. You say novels don't earn much but that's not true for somebody as famous as he was. His books still sell all over the world and he left all his royalties in trust for Miranda. *I'm* her guardian. Would her father have left a will like that if he'd wanted his daughter brought up here? He didn't *like* France. Or his parents, come to that. He meant me to be her mother.'

But even as she spoke, the certainty faded from her voice. Paul looked at her as if he were sorry for her.

'Miranda's a St Martin, Holly. Legally, that's what will count.'

She said nothing. Was this nightmare really happening? Was she sitting here in this rich place to which she'd brought Miranda so stupidly, so innocently, to be told her stepdaughter wasn't hers?

'I must keep my head,' she thought. She felt like a swimmer out of sight of land. She had to reserve her strength. She was very frightened.

'I don't want to talk about this any more for the moment,' she said, and got to her feet.

He came round the desk and seized her hands. She wrenched them away and ran from the room.

She avoided the hotel for the rest of the day. Miranda, having spent the morning with Jacqueline, was going with Pierrette to St Trop that afternoon, Pierrette's parents were taking them. Feeling she couldn't bear the Rossignols, Holly took a bus to the coast. She lay on the beach in hot, hot sun, deaf to the laughter from crowds of swimmers, blind to the red and yellow wind-surfing sails floating by like flowers.

She tried to calm down. To believe that she was over-reacting, and that it wasn't necessary to panic like this. It was plain ridiculous for the St Martins to think they'd get Miranda. Everything was on Holly's side. Robert's will, the fact that he never came to France, Miranda's happy life in Richmond, the utter disinterest shown by the grandparents for nine years. Of course they couldn't succeed. But all the time she was thinking these things, she heard Paul's voice: 'Miranda's a St Martin. Legally, that's what will count.'

What was the phrase for those dreadful battles over the custody of children? The tug of love. Was it actually possible, Holly thought, staring with unseeing eyes at the sparkling sea, that Miranda would be part of anything so appalling? And then . . . the St Martins had power. They were rich, important, well-known and they were French. Holly recognised in both of them a core of hardness, a kind of adamant quality which had also been in Robert. For all Jacqueline's exhausted pose against her cushions or Christian's grave politeness, they were tough. And now she was afraid of them.

Miranda was full of her usual good spirits when she and Holly went early to bed that night. Holly put out the light and Miranda said, 'You never asked about Trop. You'd have liked it. You can eat pancakes dripping with lavender honey, and Pierrette's father bought her mother a box of *marrons glacés* because it's her saint's day, her name is Monique. I'm afraid we ate too many. Down to the second layer and rather sickish, Pierrette and me.'

With a long yawn and a sort of grunt, Miranda was asleep.

But Holly lay all night long, open-eyed, listening to the cicadas. The air was hot and still, smelling of the night lilies. She had been awake another night, that time from happiness. Now she hated this beautiful, treacherous place. All her ease of mind, her hopes for Miranda's future, her own freedom of heart and the beginning of love, had been blighted by those few words of Paul's. It was worse than if she'd run towards him and he'd hit her in the face.

When morning came and Miranda woke bright as the sun, talking non-stop through breakfast, Holly blessed the careless merry eye of nine years old which didn't notice her own quietness or pallor.

Wearing a new white sundress bought by Jacqueline, with the design of a sun on the front and a moon on the back, and with a straw hat trailing black velvet strings, Miranda soon went down to join her grandmother in the garden. Holly dressed, feeling slightly sick. She intended to avoid the garden, but downstairs was told by the porter that, 'Madame would like you to join her for coffee.' She could think of no excuse.

Jacqueline, stretched on her chaise longue, was covered with a thin, lacy shawl. She watched Miranda's capers fondly. Christian was reading the newspaper but seeing Holly stood up, bowed, and enquired if she'd slept well. He then returned to the *Figaro*.

Miranda came up behind his chair and put her straw hat on his grey head. He looked over the newspapers indulgently.

'Does it suit me, child?'

'I think you look rather like a farmer we saw yesterday. I'd quite like to be a farmer when I'm older.'

'Why is that?'

'What's French for digging about in the earth and planting things, Holly?'

68

Holly translated and Christian said to Miranda, 'Good, good. You are a true Frenchwoman.'

Jacqueline was more fretful and demanding than usual during the morning. She sighed a good deal. She asked Holly to rearrange her cushions, sent for *tisane*, a kind of tea brewed with lime flowers, complained that her head ached, her shoulder ached and she felt dizzy. Christian emerged from the *Figaro* and said he'd send for the doctor. Jacqueline agreed, looking martyred.

But Holly did not believe any of it. Twice she met a look so penetrating that it was obvious Jacqueline knew Paul had spoken to her. Holly wasn't taken in by Jacqueline's performance. It was done for her benefit, and Holly almost hated the display and the woman giving it.

'It's impossible,' thought Holly, making an excuse and going back into the hotel. 'I can't just sit and pretend he hasn't told me. *She knows*. She wants a showdown. Wants me to come into the open. Oh God, what am I going to do?'

Disobeying the caution she'd sworn to herself to act upon, she went straight up to Paul's office and knocked loudly.

The door opened.

'Holly. Is there something I can do for you?'

The question, the polite calm of his manner, his handsome, unmoved looks and air of belonging to himself filled her with anger. She brushed past him into the room and burst out, 'I must see you.'

He carefully closed the door.

'Sit down.'

'I'll stand.'

'Do sit. You're very white. Are you quite well? Let

69

me order you some coffee.'

'I don't want anything but to talk to you. Don't try to put me off. I want to talk about Miranda and tell you that what they want is out of the question. Once and for all, get it into Jacqueline St Martin's head that *it's out of the question*. I'll never give Miranda up. I'll die first.'

'Holly, don't talk in that wild way.' He was anxious and concerned. 'You're very upset and you look dreadful. I'm very, very sorry. Please don't interrupt –' as she tried to talk down the maddeningly reasonable voice – 'Of course we'll talk and it grieves me that we didn't speak more yesterday but you suddenly went away. I understand all you feel, believe me. But you're so white; you look quite ill. I beg you, sit down calmly and let me get you something.'

He came over, took her gently by the shoulder and forced her to sit down. He could feel her shaking. He rang for a waiter and ordered something, and when it came, made her drink a little. It was a kind of peach brandy.

'We make it here,' he said. He sat down at his desk, leaning towards her.

'Listen, Holly. About Miranda. Let us talk things over quietly. I'm sure that's best, but we can't do it here. Anybody might come in. Christian or Jacqueline. Even Miranda looking for you. The last thing we want, for instance, is Jacqueline barging in. Do you agree?'

'I don't want to talk to *her* about it.'

'And I don't think you should. We must get away from the Rossignols. Let me take you out tonight. Please. I'm worried too, I can't do my job for thinking about you. Look, there's a festival at Haut de la Pinède this evening, why don't we go there? Have dinner by ourselves and really talk. It would make all the difference to be out of the Rossignols. What do you say?'

'If you want to.'

'Please, Holly.'

He told her he'd see her in the private garden at half-past seven.

That night she dressed indifferently in the only expensive thing Robert had ever bought her, a white chiffon dress with small floating sleeves and a full skirt. She brushed her hair and made up her face, but it didn't hide the dark rings under her eyes. It gave her a dreary satisfaction to look at her own wan face. Why should he have a pretty companion? 'I look awful and that's how I feel.'

She was dreading this evening and yet it was a kind of miserable relief. Better than risking more of those sharp looks from Jacqueline, and fearing that the subject would suddenly burst between them.

When she came into the garden, Paul was already there. But he was not alone. A girl was standing with him.

'You're very punctual, Holly. May I present Anne-Marie de Lambruche?'

The girl put out a graceful hand. She was taller than Holly but not as thin, with a rather voluptuous figure, a face with a pointed chin and narrow eyes. She had a mass of russet-blonde hair and reminded Holly of a fox.

'A pleasure to meet you, madame.'

That middle-aged title again. Tired and unhappy, Holly still resented it.

71

'Jacqueline has been telling me about the grand-daughter from London. She raves. She's quite boring on the subject,' said Anne-Marie with a giggle.

Her English was as good as Paul's, she had a face full of vivacious life, her eyes shone maliciously. Holly answered briefly. Was the girl a friend of Paul's? she wondered. How long would she hang about here? All that Holly wanted was to go away from the hotel, somewhere to talk to Paul alone. She felt rather faint from sleeplessness and so nervous that she was slightly sweating. The only bearable thing was to talk the misery out. Why wouldn't that girl go?

But Anne-Marie settled down to enjoy herself. Reposing on Jacqueline's chaise longue, she spread orchid-coloured skirts, and batted the conversation along with Paul, now and then including Holly with a laughing question or a joke. Mostly, she and Paul spoke of people Holly didn't know. Holly saw that Paul was in a difficulty. 'But why doesn't he just say straight out that we have to go?' thought Holly. She detested all this French politeness, it was a sort of macabre dance.

Anne-Marie finally leaned forward and looked at Holly, saying with girlish charm, 'Paul told me he's taking you to Haut de la Pinède. Would you think me dreadful if I begged to come too? I was supposed to be going with a friend but he's had to fly to Lyon on business. He's always doing things like that.'

A pout like Jacqueline's.

'He won't be back until the weekend, and I do adore the Pinède festival!' A deprecating smile. 'So . . . would you think me awful if I invited myself along?'

72

Holly didn't look at Paul.

The French girl made a big drama of insisting that she must sit at the back of the car. They set off into the dark countryside, not on the broad roads to the coast, but climbing a hill towards pine forests. When they were high, the air was chill and smelled of pines, and when Paul drove down into steep dips, the chill disappeared, the air grew warm and was scented with herbs growing in the rock-scattered valleys.

After a while they left the hills and a river gorge and came into a gentle countryside, with large houses in cultivated gardens of drooping trees and the blue flash of swimming pools. Restaurants were cheerful with lights and parked cars. Then they were back in the dark country again. Anne-Marie leaned forward.

'There you are, madame. Haut de la Pinède, beloved of the tourists, who think it's like a movie.'

Crowning a hill, glittering with lights, the village rose suddenly as if set on a rock in the sea of vineyards. Paul parked at the bottom of the hill among lines of cars.

'I'm afraid I shall totter, Paul,' said Anne-Marie, climbing from the car. 'It's my stupid shoes, but men keep telling me they're so sexy.'

She exhibited a long, suntanned leg and a shoe consisting of nothing but silver straps fine as the thinnest string, with a heel so high it was remarkable she could balance on it. Even unsuspicious Holly knew she was referring to Holly's own flat-heeled sandals.

Haut de la Pinède was a hill village like Vanergues, guarded by great walls and approached by a steep road. Crowds were climbing the hill and Holly could hear music, a thump of drums, a wail of fifes or some such wind instrument. Paul walked between the girls; Anne-Marie chatted, Holly was silent. Her spirits were at zero. She had no stomach for gaiety, festivals, crowds, indeed for anything but trying to cope with misery. Paul took her arm. He gave it a slight pressure as if to say – I agree, I wish we were alone, but what can we do?

The village walls, castellated like a medieval fortress, were hung with banners which Anne-Marie greeted with derision.

'Aha, the arms of the local nobility. That's a joke. In Burgundy we don't accept one of those old Provençal titles. They simply invented them. Imagine that, madame!'

'Anne-Marie, don't be a snob; we are supposed to be republicans,' said Paul mildly, getting a burst of laughter for a reply.

Children were selling rosemary in the village, little bunches tied with mauve ribbon. Paul bought two, and when he gave one to Anne-Marie she said he was treating her like a tourist. The crowds eventually arrived in the square which was the centre of the pageant. About fifty people were forming into a procession. There were young and older men, women, girls and excited children, all dressed in costumes of the oddest variety. There were men in armour, boys in short jackets and white knee breeches, girls in striped skirts and embroidered aprons, others in royal velvet with ermine-edged trains. Some wore straw hats, some wigs, some helmets, one or two wore crowns. Men carried spears. Boys tooted on recorders. The procession took itself seriously, and there was scarcely a smile under wobbling helmets or gilt tiaras. The crowd applauded and threw flowers.

Anne-Marie pushed her way into the front row and beckoned so violently that Paul and Holly had to join her. She said in a loud whisper, 'How ridiculous people look in costume when they are not actors! See that man in armour over there? He works at the cleaners. Wouldn't you *know* it?'

'Be quiet, Anne-Marie. He'll hear you.'

'Paul, how stupid you are, now who speaks English among the villagers at La Pinède?'

The procession began to move and the crowds followed. It made its way to the war memorial where flowers were laid and music played. Then to a bronze bust of a General in the uniform of the French foreign legion. He had a wreath of carnations hooked round his neck by a girl in ermine and a crown.

'He's La Pinède's great hero; the square is named after him,' said Paul to Holly.

With the ceremonies completed, the band stopped thumping out its music, the procession melted and the costumed figures disappeared into the town hall. The crowds went into restaurants and cafés. Paul looked up at the town clock.

'I think we ought to hurry. Our table's booked for nine.'

Anne-Marie wasn't listening. She had stopped outside a boutique whose window was full of hand-embroidered cotton dresses.

'See that one in the corner, Paul? Isn't it exactly my blue? I simply must ask how much it is.'

She walked off, and went into the shop. Paul glanced at Holly and said after a moment, 'Look, do you think you could stay with her? If you don't she'll be hours; I know Anne-Marie. I really should go and make sure of our table. On festival nights everywhere's packed and we could lose it.'

Holly briefly agreed. 'But does Anne-Marie know where we're going?'

'The Mûrs d'Argent, she knows it well. See you in a few minutes then. Do your best to hurry her up, could you?'

With his swift, graceful walk, he moved away and disappeared round a corner. Holly knew very well that he had left on purpose, to avoid being alone with her. With Anne-Marie temporarily out of the way, the inevitable conversation about Miranda would begin. And when the French girl reappeared it would come to a too-obvious stop. Holly supposed that he was being clever. She didn't want him to be clever. Nor did she want to be in the company of the girl now in deep conversation with the young woman who owned the boutique. Anne-Marie discussed prices, appeared surprised that they were so high, and blandly requested the owner to take four dresses out of the window.

'Come and tell me which you think suits me best,' said Anne-Marie to Holly, going to the back of the shop. The changing cubicle was scarcely large enough for one. Anne-Marie pointed at a stool, and Holly was forced to sit squashed against the wall.

Anne-Marie proceeded to try on one exquisite dress after another. All were made of thinnest white lawn, embroidered with variously-coloured chains of flowers. One dress had pale brown embroidery, another lemon yellow, another a soft shade of greenish blue. Tying belts, examining buttonholes, Anne-Marie studied herself critically in the glass.

'This blue is too washed-out looking. It has no strength.'

Buttoning a sleeve, she remarked à propos of nothing, 'The little stepdaughter is a success, isn't she? Do you enjoy being a mother? Paul says you're only twenty-five.'

Pressed against the wall, Holly said coolly that she liked looking after Miranda very much. Anne-Marie ran her fingers through her reddish hair. She looked more like a fox than ever.

'Naturally I've heard the big news. That the St Martins plan to keep the child.'

Holly froze.

'I'm sorry Paul told you that.'

'Why? Everybody will know soon enough. Anyway, it wasn't Paul, it was Jacqueline going on about what a little St Martin the child was and how enchanted she and Christian are with her.'

'Everybody's fond of Miranda. She's lovely.'

'No, she's not, she's plain. But one can see she might be not unattractive when she grows up. They want to make her their heiress. She'll inherit a *lot* of francs, lucky little monkey.'

'I've no intention of allowing her to stay in France. I haven't spoken to the St Martins about this and I don't wish to talk about it to you.' Holly was seriously angry.

Anne-Marie made a 'goodness, listen to you!' face and took off the dress, only to slip into another. She was not in the least put out.

Setting her brilliant hair to rights again, she said, 'I suppose you're playing for time. It won't work, you know.'

Holly's heart beat fast. She knew she should freeze

into silence but her alarm was too strong.

'I won't give her up. They'll have to accept that. Paul will help me.'

Anne-Marie burst out laughing. She really laughed, as somebody might at a farce. She dabbed her eyes.

'You can't be serious. But I see that you are. Really, madame, that's very rich. *Paul* help you? Did he say so? It's too bad of him.'

'What do you mean?'

It was the question Anne-Marie wanted. She gave a smile which didn't bother to conceal its malice.

She busied herself for a moment changing into the dress embroidered in blue for a second time. Holly thought, 'I must stop this conversation somehow.' But it was already too late, for Anne-Marie's tawny head emerged from the dress, and she was already talking as she pulled the folds expertly into place.

'Don't tell me you haven't heard the gossip by now? Everybody learns everything in Vanergues far too soon in my opinion. Someone must have told you all about Paul and Sally St Martin.'

She paused. She knew very well what she was doing.

'That's right, isn't it, her name was Sally? I never knew her, of course – before my time – and it all happened ages ago when Robert brought her here. They were engaged then. *Well* . . .' said Anne-Marie, 'we have a phrase in French for a certain kind of love – we call it the lightning strike. That's exactly how it was with Sally and Paul. They were positively struck, went around together the entire time. They were inseparable. Apparently Robert St Martin was furious with jealousy and, as for Jacqueline, you can

78

just imagine how she took it!'

Looking at her own reflection in the glass, Anne-Marie continued to talk.

'One can imagine that an Englishwoman would be knocked out by Paul: he's so good-looking in the very French manner. Anyway, Robert St Martin soon took her back to England and they were married. But, guess what. Miranda was born at *exactly* the right time afterwards. Everybody at Vanergues thought that so interesting!'

She turned to Holly with another smile.

'So, we ask, who is the father of the little heiress? But we know the answer. It amazes me that you hadn't heard all this. I'm sure you're glad to know it now, because of what you said earlier about Paul helping you. You see how that couldn't happen. Paul is the last person to do a thing for you, madame, if you try to keep the child and return with her to England.'

She pulled off the final lawn dress and zipped herself back into her orchid-coloured silk. Then, picking up the discarded cotton dresses in an untidy bundle, she walked out of the cubicle.

The boutique owner was hovering.

Anne-Marie dumped the clothes on a chair.

'Thank you. But I'm afraid although I've tried them all, there isn't one that's right for my shade of hair. I always have such difficulty, you know, getting the exact tone of blue or green. Even the coffee shades aren't what I'm looking for.'

She walked out of the shop, calling to Holly over her shoulder to hurry.

'Paul is going to get bored if we keep him waiting any longer.'

Catching her up and accompanying her across the square, down a narrow street, and finally up a flight of stone steps into a restaurant, Holly had the extraordinary sensation that a knife had been put into her ribs. She could feel it and the sickish pain following.

Paul settled them at a table, the waiter came to take their order and Anne-Marie began to discuss the food. Holly made an effort to pull herself together. She tried to think about something else, looked about and concentrated on unimportant things. They were in a great vaulted room with a painted ceiling and windows built into the ramparts of the old village. The tables were in long lines, very crowded, and people were enjoying themselves, eating, drinking, laughing, flirting. Holly noticed a vase of red roses and, quite near it, a girl with brilliant blue eyes. She tried to take things in . . .

The whole evening was like that. Now and again during dinner Paul looked at her with concern, and two or three times he remarked that she was very quiet and eating almost nothing.

'Perhaps she's slimming; I always am,' said Anne-Marie airily. 'Leave her in peace, not everybody likes gabbing away as I do. I must tell you all my news from home, Paul, it is months since we met, isn't it? And not a card do you send. You know the frost ruined our vines in Burgundy? You're so lucky, our weather was filthy. I can't *tell* you how Papa and Georges carried on about the vines, and the losses, and exports, and the figures on their beastly computers. Computers. You'd think them more important than our grapes. Georges flew to London and Birmingham and some other English cities. Apparently the English drink wine now. I thought –'

to Holly – 'they drank tea.'

'We still do.'

'But lots of wine as well which pleases my family, and when Georges arrived in Birmingham . . .'

She talked on. Her voice was light and laughing, and she seemed to amuse Paul. Holly was silent. She thought, 'Perhaps it is a lie and she's the sort of girl who enjoys making trouble. She looked delighted when she told me that story. How horrible her expression was. I knew she took a dislike to me when we first met, and then when she saw I was upset over Miranda she decided to make it worse.

'Yet,' thought Holly, 'it isn't impossible. Suppose Paul is Miranda's father?' She thought of Sally's face in the painting at home in Richmond. For all the dead woman's fashionable beauty, the artist had put a certain hardness into that face. If Sally had taken it into her head to have a love affair with Paul, might that not have made Robert's passion all the stronger, the more jealous and possessive? He had married Sally. But a past affair, wounding, unforgotten, could explain part of that permanent sorrow, for Sally had not been wholly his.

Worse than thoughts of the dead past was what this fact could do the threat of Holly losing Miranda. She dared not think about that yet.

Anne-Marie was too practised to monopolise the conversation with a man for long, and she persuaded Paul into talking about the Bavarian Hotel, the Goldener Hirsch. Holly tried to listen as he described the country there, the fast rivers and thick forests. The hotel was in a Bavarian town where an archduke in the eighteenth century had built a little theatre. 'It is baroque gone crazy,' Paul said, 'with double eagles and crowns all over a royal box and gilt candelabra ten feet high.' The hotel was gothic, far older than the theatre. It was beamed and carved, in summer a pool in the garden was full of water-lilies, in winter there were huge open fires.

Anne-Marie made up for Holly's silence with her interest and comment. She was going ski-ing at Christmas to Germany, she said, she simply must spend a few days at the Goldener Hirsch, and Paul would telephone beforehand and make sure she had a very special room, wouldn't he? Talking, laughing, she began to take the sugar lumps from a bowl on the coffee tray. They were wrapped in paper patterned with dominoes, with different colours and numbers. She lined them up on the table and made him play dominoes with her. She looked at him coquettishly, her reddish-gold hair falling across her brow.

'How bad you are at games. I've won.'

Unwrapping the final domino, she ate it.

Even a nightmare does not last for ever and the time came for them to leave the restaurant. Paul drove them back by moonlight. It was nearly one o'clock when Holly said goodnight.

'Come and see me off, Paul,' said Anne-Marie, vaguely offering Holly her hand.

When Holly went into the hotel, a few people were still lingering on a sofa under a large photograph of Picasso, drinking and talking in the low voices of late hours. It seemed strange to her to see faces actually happy.

She went to the reception and said to the old porter, 'Have you a telephone downstairs? I don't want to disturb my stepdaughter.'

'But of course, madame.' He took her to the

distant room called the library which was rarely used. Beyond it there was an alcove with a telephone and a table.

'You'll be undisturbed here,' the old porter said. 'Give me the number, madame, and I'll put it through for you from Reception.'

She sat down and waited. Picking up the receiver she heard the number ringing in London. 'Oh, do be there. Please be there.' A click. A man's voice.

'Hello?'

'Mike, it's Holly. I'm *so sorry* to ring so late.'

'Petal! How nice and what a surprise. Surely you're not back already?'

'No, no, we're still in France.'

'Great to hear from you. How's it all going?'

'Oh Mike, something so awful has happened, I felt I had to talk to you –'

She poured out the story, omitting only what Anne-Marie had told her that night; she felt she couldn't bear to tell him that. But she repeated what Paul had said to her and how frightened she was of what the St Martins would do. As the words tumbled out she kept saying, 'They can't take her away, can they?' She said she didn't know who to turn to.

'Turn to me, Petal. And cheer up, it can't be as bad as all that, because nothing ever is. Your husband meant you to have custody of Miranda. It's monstrous, what's going on. Those people haven't clapped eyes on her since she was born. Now they ask you both out for their thrash and all of a sudden it's "let's keep the child". It's outrageous. Are you very upset?'

'Yes.'

'You don't sound so good, poor Petal. Now listen. The first thing is – give me your telephone number. Like an idiot I clean forgot to ask when we said goodbye.'

She gave it to him.

'Right. I'll think about everything and give you a buzz tomorrow or the day after. Incidentally what's the name of the hotel? Didn't Miranda say it's called the house of parrots or something?'

'Nightingales,' said Holly and smiled for the first time that day.

'OK, I'll ring you. In the meantime stay cool. I mean it, Petal, don't say or do *anything* no matter how much you want to have a showdown. There are times when it's absolutely essential not to show your hand. I know what I'm talking about. It can be very, very smart in business not to let the other guy know what you're up to. So you'll stay cool, won't you?'

'It's so hard. But yes, I will.'

'Good girl. I'll be ringing you very soon.'

She rang off. There had been a few minutes of relief while she was talking to him. But she felt no safer, no less anxious and afraid.

As she was asking for her key at Reception, she saw Paul come through the door. She pretended not to, but he came straight over to her.

'That was a very curious evening, Holly.'

She didn't reply.

'I was going to ask you to have a nightcap with me, but you look tired. You've been so quiet. And we haven't had the chance to say a word about that other thing, have we?'

'And I don't want to,' she thought, 'I wish I could get away from you. I wish I was in England *now*.'

He stood, his hands in his pockets, looking at her for a moment. A thin girl in a thin dress.

'How quiet you've been,' he said again. 'Are you worried?'

Mike had asked that question, too. So differently. Now Mike's warning was in her ears and she managed a level, 'I'm perfectly all right. But, as you say, I do feel quite tired.'

She made a move to go and he walked with her to the staircase.

'You're very pale, Holly.'

He took her hand and, as she'd dreaded, gave it his casual butterfly kiss. Still holding her hand he said, 'Trust me.'

She went up the stairs without looking back.

4

For hours through the hot Mediterranean night she thought about what Anne-Marie had told her. How degrading scandal was, to the teller, the audience, and to the object of the scandal. Anne-Marie had smeared Paul with mud but her hands were no cleaner, and Holly herself felt defiled even for having listened.

At first she tried to put it out of her mind, and then, when that proved impossible, simply to refuse to believe it. But she couldn't. It could easily and hideously be true. And if Paul *were* Miranda's father, everything in this terrible situation was traced back to him.

It was clear that he had a lot of influence over Jacqueline St Martin who respected and admired him, even doted on him rather as she did on Miranda. Holly had often seen how her eyes followed him, the way her face vividly altered when she caught sight of him. Perhaps Paul, after all this time, had begun to think about his own child and had decided to see her. It would be easy enough to persuade the St Martins to make a move towards Miranda and Holly, particularly for the anniversary celebrations. And it was Paul who'd come over to England, bringing the invitation.

The French core of it, Holly thought, was money. Miranda would eventually inherit more than half the St Martin hotels. The couple were getting old and Paul had great talent in this rich business. When he'd met Miranda, he'd seen just how English she was. That had made his mind up. He wasn't prepared to risk half his business being inherited by an English girl. She might want to sell her share to people Paul didn't want. It happened that businesses were damaged, even ruined, when outsiders inherited a part of them. So Paul had made up his mind to keep Miranda in Provence under his eye and under his influence. She was to be reared as a Frenchwoman.

Holly lay awake trying to face the worse. The quiet night dragged by.

Then sometime in the dawn, when a sleepy bird began to chirp and a greyish light was filtering down the edges of the curtains, she saw her way out.

'I won't stay. I'll take Miranda home at once. It will all be different when we're back in Richmond. *They'll* find it very difficult when we are in our own country. We'll be safer, and we'll be away from them.' The thought of leaving Paul, whose dangerous company both drew and frightened her, was the strongest relief of all. After she had made up her mind to leave the Rossignols at once, she fell asleep.

'Holly, *petit déjeuner* is here, do wake up!'

It was Miranda tugging at her hand. Holly opened her eyes to see the impish face bent over her.

'You were *so* asleep. I tried to wake you by singing but you didn't budge. Come and eat. I'm starving.'

Holly climbed wearily out of bed and went on to

the balcony. The sun was shining. The fresh bright air seemed to glitter.

'Guess what,' said Miranda, helping herself to black cherry jam. 'Pierrette and me saw a real nightingale yesterday. It was outside the village. We did, honestly. It was perched on a bush, a brownish bird with a reddish tail, it's quite like a robin. I knew what it was, and Pierrette's father looked it up afterwards and said I was right. It was singing, too. Pierrette said people sometimes shoot them and eat them. Isn't it awful? I said we belonged to the Royal Society for the Protection of Birds and she'd better join and we could fix it for her when we get home. I'm sure her Dad would pay, he likes birds.'

'We'll write when we get home,' said Holly, pouring coffee. Then, without emphasis, 'Miranda, I think we ought to get back right away.'

Miranda had been looking over the balcony, trying to spy her favourite waiter. She spun round.

'*Home. Go home!* Why?'

'We've been here two weeks, more than that, and it will give us a chance to have some time in Richmond before term begins.'

'But term's not for ages! We came over for the grandparents' party. Holly, you promised we'd stay for the party. You promised!'

Brown eyes brimmed. The face was a mask of woe.

'Darling, I'm sorry but I've changed my mind. It's no good arguing. I don't think we should stay any longer, and that's all there is to it. Now, finish your breakfast and go down to the pool. Didn't you say Pierrette was coming early this morning? I've got to pack.'

'Fortunately, at that moment Pierrette appeared, already in her bikini. Holly said swiftly, 'Miranda, don't mention what I've just said for the moment, please. I haven't told your grandmother yet. Don't say anything until I tell you.'

Rushing over, Miranda gave her a strangling hug. 'Change your mind. Oh do!'

She ran out of the room with Pierrette.

Holly fetched the suitcases from a cupboard and put them on her bed. It comforted her to look at them, battered old things which had belonged to her mother. She thought of where she kept them in the Richmond attic, and the look of the attic with grey light filtering through the barred window. When she opened them, they smelled of home. Home! She would be there today, among friends she understood and in the world where she wasn't frightened all the time.

Then she thought about leaving the Rossignols. Leaving Paul. She'd known him only a short time, and there had been moments when he had made her so happy she had thought her heart would burst. 'I suppose it was love,' she thought. The beginnings of love. Stupidly and blissfully she had believed he felt as she did. He had looked at her sometimes as if he knew, almost owned, something in her deepest self. She'd thought that although he wanted her physically he had desired more than that, some completeness which they both felt when they were together. The longing, as old as humans were, to be one person, one soul. That was what she had believed, wonderfully happy as she had been, held close in the arms of an enemy.

Folding Miranda's dresses, she began to put them

into the suitcase. There were so many new ones. If the rest of the summer in London happened to be cold, Miranda would need more cardigans . . . There was a knock at the door. It must be the chambermaid come to collect the tray. With her back to the door, busy with the packing, Holly called, 'Come in.'

She heard the door open.

A voice exclaimed, 'What on earth are you doing?'

It was Paul.

'You can see what I'm doing. Packing.'

She turned round, facing him like a creature at bay.

He shut the door carefully and came into the room.

'You can't do this.'

'I am doing it. We are leaving today on the first flight we can get. I have already told Miranda.'

He looked at her in grim silence.

Then, 'Holly, I beg you. Don't.'

'I'm sorry.'

She put the final dress into the case and slammed it shut. She began on her own clothes, taking dresses off hangers, rolling sandals in tissue paper. She was nervous and turned her back on him so as not to see his face. She continued to pack. He came over, and gently took the sandals out of her hands.

'What you propose to do is impossible. Surely you see that.'

'What are you talking about? Jacqueline invited us here to stay and we came and now we are going home and that's an end to it. Who is to stop us? I shall make some excuse. I'll say I'm not well or Miranda isn't or that we're needed at home. I shall think of something perfectly feasible and she'll just have to put up with it.'

His cheeks were slightly flushed. He stared at her.

'You mean you intend not to be here for their celebration? To come over for a week or two and then calmly leave before the party as if Miranda were no relation to them at all. You can't be as unfeeling as that.'

'What sort of *relation* was she to them in the last nine years?' answered Holly fiercely, thinking, 'And what sort of father were you?'

The harshness of her usually soft voice, the violence of her manner, affected him. He took hold of her hands, she pulled them away, but he was stronger than she and forced her to sit down on the bed. He sat facing her, still holding her hands in his large, powerful ones.

'I beg you to listen. What you want to do is very sudden and very cruel. Surely you know that Jacqueline is not strong and hasn't been well for many days now? Things upset her, even small things, let alone something like this. It will be the most terrible shock to her. She'll be heartbroken. You will make her ill, Holly, I'm convinced of it. I know you're worried about her wanting to keep Miranda, but nothing is settled. Nothing as serious as that can be settled in a short time. Meanwhile, have a little kindness. The poor woman has never done you any harm, and she is your husband's mother. She loves Miranda. How are you going to feel if you do go back to England now, and I telephone to say that Jacqueline has been taken seriously ill? Don't risk such a thing. *Please.*'

He let her go at last. She was silent. A struggle was going on in her heart; it was the same situation all

91

over again from the time she'd first met him and he'd persuaded her to go against her instincts and to come here. Now the fight was between her desperate longing to get away, and a fear that what he'd just said was true. Would it really make Jacqueline ill if they left now? Dared she take such a risk? If she were ill, Holly would be responsible.

'What are you thinking, Holly?'

'That you force me to do things.'

'I only asked you to be kind.'

Silence.

'I wish we'd never seen this place.'

'I can't wish that. You and I would never have met.'

'Oh, don't be nice to me now, Paul. Not now of all times.'

'What does that mean? That you intend to leave in spite of what I've told you?'

'I wish I could.'

His whole figure – tensed, intent – relaxed. He stood up.

'You won't regret it. Thank you.'

When he had gone she slowly unpacked and as slowly went down the stairs and into the private garden, looking for Miranda to tell her what she'd decided. Poor child, ignorant of all that was happening. She would be pleased.

Miranda, said Jacqueline languidly from her chaise longue, had left with Pierrette.

'I told them to go on swimming in the hotel pool, but no, they must swim in Pierrette's, it seems. I said why. It is far smaller than ours here. But you know how it is with children. They kept giggling in a foolish way and whispering to each other. They have these silly ideas. Sit down, Holly. I will order your coffee. Or would you prefer some of my tisane?'

Jacqueline indicated a chair beside her with the air of somebody who wasn't to be refused.

After her scene with Paul, Holly found that her mind simply wasn't working. She couldn't think of a single excuse and she thought, 'Oh God, suppose she starts talking about Miranda now? What shall I say? How can I stop her? Mike said to say nothing but how can I?' Holly had never had an enemy in her life. Now it seemed as if the Rossignols was filled with them, from Paul literally stopping her escape just now to this woman with her painted probing blue eyes.

But Holly, taut as a violin string, heard Jacqueline merely begin to gossip about the party.

'It's going to be much larger than we planned. *Tiens*, we have so many friends! And one can't hurt their feelings when they are simply longing to be asked. What a lot of work our celebration is going to be. However, we have Paul in charge. That's something Christian and I are so thankful for. Paul has true flair for big occasions like this.'

Her gossip turned to Miranda's clothes, to shopping expeditions, and she repeated an impertinent remark of her grand-daughter's with an indulgent laugh.

'Do you know, I remember Robert behaving like that when he was about ten. He used to have that same wicked look in his eyes. Mischievous. Christian always says I have mischief in my nature, and Robert and Miranda both inherited it from me.'

'I am sorry if she wasn't very polite, Madame St Martin. I must speak to her about it.'

Jacqueline looked at her sweetly.

'Now you can scarcely take any responsibility, my dear. It is I, and Christian, and her poor father, of course, who are the reason for the little one's character. Her French blood is so evident. She has temperament. I saw that right away. She's a real St Martin. There is the way she talks and that certain tone of voice . . .'

Holly scarcely listened. It was so odd to be sitting here in the garden with Jacqueline, listening to her boast about family resemblances. Miranda might not be a St Martin at all. Perhaps she was a result of that lightning-strike, as Anne Marie had called it, that brief and violent affair between Sally and Paul. Yet Holly knew that what Jacqueline said about Miranda's Southern blood was still true, for Paul was from this part of the world too. Miranda's gift for French, that gleam of temperament which showed far more since she had come here, were as inherited as those large, dark brown eyes. But from whom?

Jacqueline chatted on, not crudely spelling it out but rather airily indicating that she was making plans, 'just silly ideas you know,' for Miranda's future. 'We might talk about a trip to Paris.' she said, vaguely gesturing.

'They're certain that they're going to get her,' thought Holly. Perhaps a lawyer has spoken to them. Or Paul went to see one. For a moment, in a detached almost unemotional way, Holly looked at the women lying near her, at the bright face and figure weakly stretched out. 'I don't believe she is ill,' Holly thought. 'Oh, why did I let him talk me into staying?' But he'd faced her with the classic dilemma which dares not risk terrible consequences. Even if she disbelieved it, she couldn't ignore Jacqueline's ill health. Paul had made it impossible for them to leave yet. What did she mean, 'yet'? Perhaps Miranda would never return home again.

Holly eventually saw the opportunity to make an excuse about some letters to catch the post. Jacqueline disinterestedly agreed, sharpening up as Holly left to ask if Holly would remember to see that Miranda changed into her new denim dress, please? Lately Jacqueline had developed the habit of dictating what her grand-daughter should wear, and always clothes that she herself had bought.

The porter told Holly that Pierrette's parents had telephoned to say Miranda would be spending the afternoon with them. They would bring her back to the Rossignols at six.

Holly ate no lunch. She sat at the furthest end of the terrace under an olive tree, cutting a slice of melon into small squares, and drinking iced Vichy water. She tried to concentrate on the one good thing which had happend in the last few days – she'd talked to Mike Armstrong. He was clever. He might think of some way of helping her. Then back went her thoughts to a desperate, almost primitive longing to escape.

The lunchtime hours went by. The afternoon was very hot and, as people finished their meal, they wandered off into the hotel, towards their rooms and the long enchanted sleep of the South. Holly could no more imagine being able to sleep at present than she could remember what it had felt like, a few short days ago, to be filled with joy. She thought, with dry amusement, that there was a good old

English solution to unhappiness. To go for a walk.

Up in her room, she fetched a straw hat, then went down to ask the porter if he could suggest a country walk somewhere outside the village. He raised an eyebrow at the idea at this time of day, but gave her some directions.

She walked slowly away from the hotel. Outside in the streets it was hotter than ever, but the walls threw inky passages of shade and she dived into them as if into water. All the houses were asleep; the afternoon silence seemed to ring. She thought, 'How full of flowers it is everywhere, you'd think it a happy place.' From the windows great shawls of geraniums fell in masses, all budding and opening and flowering and dropping their crimson petals at the same time.

Leaving the village behind, she took the long hill downwards into the valley, then turned along a road where large houses were set back, hidden in gardens behind eucalyptus trees whose long, dark branches hung like screens. The porter had said she must look for a turning away on the right. It was more than a mile in the dazzling sun, but at last she found it. There was a road which climbed again, a road so narrow that two cars could not have passed each other. Insects buzzed on the grassy banks, never as loud as her stinging thoughts.

The country road climbed and climbed, passing fields planted with the thick tufts of cultivated lavender, and others high with cultivated sunflowers turning their discs to the sky. At last she came to a great plateau. Mile after mile of lonely scrubland spread ahead of her towards the far blue distances where along the horizon was the long, uneven line of the Maritime Alps.

Holly walked across the grass. It was short and pale as silver, starred with tiny, unfamiliar flowers and hovering with butterflies. The air shimmered. A faint breeze blew which she never felt in the ravined streets of Vanergues.

Looking down at the flowers – mauve, white, sprays of pure blue – smelling the scent of Provence on the soft wind, it seemed to Holly a kind of sin that a country so exquisite should be so cruel. Provence ought to be as beautiful as it seemed. Nothing was. Nobody was. Least of all Paul.

The meadows gently sloped to a dip and then rose in a series of terraces planted with very old olive trees. It looked invitingly cool in their shade. Beyond the olives she could see the half-hidden shape of a stone house which looked as old as they were. She wondered if anybody still lived there. This country had many ruins like that, overgrown and sad. People had gone away and never come back.

The sun blazed down; she longed to sit under the distant olive trees, solitary, with her thoughts in the shadows. But, as she came nearer, she saw that there was a barrier between herself and the terraces. It was a great yellow forest of bamboo which in Provence they called cannis, grown over ten feet high. 'Surely there must be a path through all that,' she thought and, still looking towards the trees, she quickened her step.

Just then she imagined she heard a voice far off behind her. She didn't turn to look. The last thing she wanted to see was a group of people cheerfully invading the loneliness. She thirsted to be alone, to sit in the shade and think, think what she must do

97

next. The voice shouted again. Again she ignored it.

'Holly! Holly!'

She couldn't believe she was hearing her own name. A man still some distance away was running towards her. It was Paul.

She had a strong desire to run too. Away from him and from everything that was happening because of him. If it were not for Paul she would be with Miranda at the airport by now. But something urgent in the running figure stopped her. When he reached her, he was sweating.

'I don't remember the last time I actually ran in August,' he said, panting. 'It's distinctly hot.'

'What do you want?'

His breathing slowed down.

'Don't sound so sharp. May we sit for a moment, please? This isn't the weather for jogging.'

Thinning her lips, she sat down on the grass. It was burning hot and starred with flowers.

'What do you want?' she said again.

'You'll be slightly more grateful when I tell you. I came to warn you. François, the old idiot, said he'd suggested you could come for a walk here, near the Ferme de Manosque.'

'Is that the old house?'

'Yes. It's empty. Falling to pieces. It hasn't been occupied for a hundred years. Only the scorpions live there.'

'I wouldn't have gone inside.'

'That's not the point. What Francois *didn't* tell you is that you can't get through to it anyway because of the swamp.' He gestured towards the bamboo. 'It looks harmless enough and there are a number of old pathways which one or two of the

farmers know how to use. But it's extremely dangerous. People have got into difficulties there.'

She was very taken aback.

'I didn't fancy the idea of you being swallowed in
gurgling mud. It's like a quicksand. One just can't
extricate oneself.'

She took this in. Apparently she owed him something. Her life?

'Thank you for warning me,' she said stiffly.

'*De rien.*'

'It isn't nothing. You had to run.'

'So I did. Hot work.'

She looked pale under the shadow of the big straw
hat. It seemed to have drained away her sunburn.
She sat as he'd often seen her do before, awkwardly,
gawkily, like a tall boy. All the peaceful humour was
gone from her face.

She said perversely, 'I don't see how mud can
gurgle anywhere as dry as this.'

'You must believe me. There's an underground
spring which feeds wells miles away. There's a very
deep marsh under all that cannis. Years ago somebody who lived at the farm was drowned in the mud.
His body was never found.'

'How horrible.'

'Yes. Horrible things can happen if you don't
know of the danger.'

'And even if you do,' she couldn't stop saying. She
saw the shot go home.

He picked at the flowering grasses, bending his
head, his handsome face in shadow. He understood
her very well. He knew it scared her to remain at the
Rossignols and yet he'd made her. It had been black-
mail of a kind. He'd played the old powerful hand,

one to disturb her conscience. He felt guilty. And not guilty. Holly said not a word, but her silence did.

Glancing at his watch, he always seemed conscious of time, he said that he must get back.

'The builder is coming to repair one of the roofs. He has to climb right up and crawl across, replacing any broken tiles and rearranging those which are misplaced. When there's a strong wind, the Mistrale or the Tramontana from Italy, the old tiles break or lift and the roof leaks.'

'Always something.'

'In a hotel, yes. I daresay you find it in your house at Richmond too.'

'What a ridiculous conversation,' she thought. 'We sound like people who can't think of a thing to say. Well, I can't. I don't trust him.' She thought how the way he looked was still so intensely and painfully attractive. Something physically strong in him, his muscular arms, the line of his jaw, his shoulders, his whole body – and, more than physical things, his personality which belonged to itself, excited her gentle, feminine soul. How was it possible still to feel so, knowing what she did?

He began to saunter beside her, very slowly, across the great sun-filled meadows.

'I said I'd stay because of what you told me this morning, but the thing is still hanging over Miranda and me,' she blurted out. 'We said we'd talk.'

She wished she hadn't said it. Mike had told her not to.

'So I did.'

'Well?'

'Well, then,' he said casually, 'let's talk.'

100

She lost her temper.

'How can you sound like that? You know very well, or if you had any heart you would, how I'm feeling. You know I wish to heaven I could leave now. This minute. Today! You're cold and horrible. Don't you at least have the imagination to realise what this is doing to me? You –'

She was in full flood but he suddenly pulled her to him and kissed her. He kissed her violently, stopping her mouth with his, stopping her talking, pressing her so close that she couldn't breathe, embracing her hard but without tenderness. It was hateful and she fought to escape but he only went on kissing her more forcibly than ever. She couldn't get away until he let her go, and when he did she tripped over. He pulled her to her feet as roughly as if she were a man.

With a sob she began to run, reaching the lane and rushing down the hill as if pursued by demons. He called, 'Stop!' but she ran on, her heart hammering, her cheeks scarlet from the heat. Breathless and panting with exhaustion, she reached the village at last, diving through a gateway and round a corner. She hid in the shadows and waited. Soon she heard footsteps. It must be Paul. He took the main street towards the hotel, and only when the steps had faded into silence did she walk back. Her head was splitting.

The maid had closed the shutters in her room, the fierce sun had been tamed to a zebra light and shade. She threw herself on the bed. Nobody had kissed her in that sexy, uncaring way since she'd been at University where drunk young man sometimes lunged. She hated him for it, she felt cheap, and he was cheapened in her own eyes. He was probably her darling Miranda's father, determined to get the child for himself. He didn't care for Miranda, only for what she represented. And, as for his feeling for herself, it made her shudder. The house of nightingales! The nightingale was a symbol of romantic midnight music, of almost unearthly happiness. This place should be renamed.

Wiping away the angry tears with the back of her hand she was faced for the second time in her life by the mystery of a man utterly unlike her idea of him. She'd married Robert in love and gratefulness, thinking she would be allowed to share his life. But he had loved only Sally. He had chosen work to replace her. He'd kept Holly out. She had never heard him say warm things except about the past; Sally's ghost, ambitious and sardonic, had haunted the Richmond house because she still possessed Robert's thoughts. Nothing about Robert had been what Holly believed when she had first loved him.

Now it had happened all over again. She had been attracted to Paul even when she first met him and he had persuaded her to change her mind and come to France. He'd convinced her that that was the right decision. His way of doing so had been clever and quick, and gentle in a way. She had soon begun to fall in love with him. And then there was the way he looked, much, much too handsome and so unaware of it. He was the most physically alluring man she had ever known. And was against her.

Tired out by her thoughts and her flight from the meadows, she fell into a restless sleep.

She woke with a start. It was six o'clock and Miranda would be back. She hastily washed her face, changed her crushed dress to a pale pink cotton, and brushed her hair. The pretty girl at Reception who had replaced old François on duty told her that Monsieur, Madame and La Demoiselle (which was how Miranda was described at the hotel) were at the pool.

The evening sun shone on the water, blazing on the oblong of turquoise blue, and the patterned tiles with their sunflowers and lizards. There were only a few swimmers in the water; it was getting late and most people had gone in to change for dinner. But three figures were standing near the diving board. Christian, Jacqueline and Miranda. Something about the trio, some curious tension in the way they stood, struck Holly with foreboding.

'Miranda?' she said, coming up to join them.

'Hi,' said Miranda, not looking at her. She was drawing a water pattern on the tiles with one toe.

'Miranda has decided to be a little English girl this evening,' said Jacqueline very coldly.

Miranda turned to Holly with an expression of exaggerated not-understanding.

'Isn't it queer, Holly, I can't understand a *single word*. At school they always say I'm no good at foreign languages.'

'Miranda don't be rude. You know perfectly well that you understand your grandmother.' Holly was shocked.

'Not a word, not a word. Worse than homework.'

'My wife bought the child a bracelet this afternoon,' said Christian heavily. 'She gave it to Miranda less than an hour ago. Miranda now says she has lost it. Or that's what I think she says. My English is not very strong. The bracelet, by the way, cost a good deal.'

'Did she drop it in the pool? We can't get her to say a word except in English,' said Jacqueline sharply.

'Miranda!' exclaimed Holly, 'What is all this nonsense about not talking French. Where *is* the bracelet?'

'I dunno. Perhaps it fell off.'

'It couldn't just fall off. Did you fasten it properly? When did you put it on? Your grandfather said it was most expensive and it was very kind of your grandmother to –'

'It wasn't kind at all. *She* liked the stupid thing. I didn't. It was all cameos or whatever they're called.'

The little girl's cheeks were crimson, and she had a strange almost wild look. Holly was alarmed. Was she ill? Had she been too long in the sun? She took her hand, but it was quite cool. Miranda clutched at Holly as if she were falling.

'What does she say? Does she remember what happened to the bracelet?' asked Christian.

'Not yet,' said Holly, and again to Miranda in English: 'You can't accept presents, especially something which cost so much –'

'I told you. I never wanted the beastly thing.'

'And then pretend it's lost,' went on Holly, making an effort to calm the disturbed child beside her.

'Tell them I don't care what happened to it. Tell them I hate all the presents they keep giving me. I hate them!' cried Miranda, just as Paul came round the corner by the rosemary hedge. He had heard every word.

'Are you refusing to speak French to your grandmother? That is very rude of you.'

His voice was stern and rather loud and it startled Miranda who clung more tightly to Holly.

104

'Apologise at once.'

Crimson to the tips of her ears, Miranda stammered an apology and rushed away, disappearing towards the hotel. Jacqueline gave a tinny laugh.

'Oh Paul, you needn't be so severe.'

She sounded pleased.

'I dislike bad behaviour.'

'But she's never like that!' burst out Holly, angry with Miranda, Paul, and most of all herself for not coping with the trouble. She was as red as her stepdaughter.

'She is now,' he said. 'She needs a firm hand and the first thing she must learn is respect for her parents.'

'Her parents!' repeated Holly, firing up.

He shrugged.

'In French, that means any relative.'

'I think I must go upstairs,' said Jacqueline, her voice suddenly quavering. 'I am unused to scenes.'

She looked pained, and Christian put a protective arm about her, leading her back into the hotel.

There was a pause. The swimmers in the pool were laughing. A girl with long, wet hair went by, climbed to the top board and executed a perfect dive.

Holly was filled with embarrassment, miserable embarrassment. Until a few minutes ago what she'd felt for Paul was anger and resentment at the way he'd kissed her, and fear because of Miranda. Bitter feelings. Now he had stopped a very unpleasant scene and it was he, not Holly, who had controlled her stepdaughter. She felt humiliated.

'Thank you for making her behave,' she said in a low voice.

'As I said, she needs a firm hand.'

'She never has until now.'

She began to walk away, but he followed her.

'You tell me she usually behaves well.'

His voice was actually accusing.

She stopped in her tracks.

'Certainly I do. And I don't care if you believe it or not.'

'Oh, I believe it.'

'What is that supposed to mean?'

'That I think it very likely your stepdaughter in England was a perfect little English miss. It occurs to me, however,' he went on in a sarcastic tone, 'that it is very convenient indeed how she's suddenly changed. She becomes very rude to her grandparents. I wonder why?'

'You mean I put her up to it.'

'I'm not a fool, Holly.'

5

'Petal?

'Mike. How good to hear you.'

'I rang earlier, but you were out. I just wanted to keep you posted with what's happening about that trouble you were telling me about.'

'What do you mean?'

'Don't sound so bothered, it all looks rather good,' he said in his brisk, businesslike voice. 'I talked to a guy I know. He's by way of being a barrister. He was very interested, as a matter of fact. I hope you don't mind if I hire him for you, just for a consultation or two? He promised he wouldn't charge an outrageous fee. Actually he owes me a favour, I sold his house for him. Well, Petal, about you. He said that things don't look at all bad. He was quite encouraging.'

'*Really*?'

'Really and truly. You've got custody. Your husband left his daughter in your care. He said that was, of course, vital. The grandparents haven't shown the least interest or sign that they wanted anything to do with Miranda until recently, which is also good for your side of the thing. This man, name of Amhurst, said you're not to worry. So just keep your hair on.'

'You mean they won't be able to take her away from me?'

Holly felt as if a huge burden had suddenly fallen off her back – like Christian in the Pilgrim's Progress when his pack fell off. She began to smile.

'What do you think of your pal Mike, then?' said her friend in London. 'The news looks good, so you can just settle down to enjoy yourself.'

'Oh, Mike, how can I thank you?'

'Don't bother your head about that, I shall think of something. As a matter of fact, I'm toying with the idea of coming over to see you.'

'Would you! Could you?'

'Yeah, I think so. There's always work to pick up in places like Nice and Cannes, and we've got contacts in both towns. And clients interested in French property. I might manage to do some work while I'm in France, as well as enjoying your company.'

'You are *kind*.'

'A friend in need, eh? I'll ring before I turn up. By the by, tell you what, see if you can fiddle me an invitation to that smart party you told me about. I like seeing how the rich live.'

'I'm sure I could manage it.'

At that moment, Holly would have promised anything.

'Great. Now you keep cheerful and you'll be seeing me sooner than you think.'

He rang off.

When Holly left the telephone she felt so happy that she could have danced. Mike was so matter-of-fact, so English, so real. How like him to want to fly out and see her. How good the news was. Suddenly she looked at everything with new eyes. She saw the

Rossignols the way she had seen it on the day of her arrival, admiring its wide terrace, its hazy views, its myriad flowers, its comfortable old walls, the faded painting of the little saint, the long passages at the end of which great pottery jars stood filled with roses.

Holly had been dreading today because the St Martins had invited her to go with them and Miranda to a beach at Cap d'Antibes. Miranda had begged Holly to come too. Lately she had become very clinging, always seeming to want Holly with her when she was with her grandparents. Perhaps it was due to the other day when Holly had said they were going to leave. It had unsettled her.

But Miranda was certainly behaving well. She produced the missing cameo bracelet with some nonsense about finding it among her swimming things. She was nice to Jacqueline. If she wasn't quite so affectionate, her grandmother did not appear to notice. And Miranda had returned to talking her remarkable, colloquial French.

The St Martins drove the girls to Cap d'Antibes. They were also accompanied, although they did not know it, by Holly's new happiness.

'I like the Garoupe beach so much more than the one where Paul swims at Juan,' remarked Jacqueline. 'How Paul can be friends with that Guy Lamartine is beyond my comprehension. He's nothing but a peasant. One must have style.'

Wearing a sundress which was too young for her, Jacqueline arrived on the smart Garoupe beach and was settled, shaded by a parasol, near her attentive husband. Christian ordered her an almond ice-cream and fussed about the angle of the parasol.

109

'You must not have a beam of the direct sunshine, chère. The doctor insisted.'

Holly moved into the direct sun and lazily oiled her suntanned arms. She watched Miranda playing with some children among the rocks in clear, greenish water. She could see exactly why Jacqueline preferred these beaches, which had elegant bars, wooden decks built right out into the water, a certain expensive look about them, and about the sunbathers lying faces turned upwards to the sun.

Suddenly Miranda gave a little cry, and began to limp back towards Holly. She showed her the sole of her foot. It was covered with tiny black thorns.

Jacqueline was horrified.

'She has stepped on a sea-urchin. Holly, you should have warned her! The spines are poisonous. Christian, go and get the car, we must take her to the infirmary at once.'

'Just a moment, chère,' said Christian, standing up. 'I have an idea where we may get some help.'

Miranda, on Holly's lap, was looking with deep interest at her own black-starred foot.

'I don't expect I shall be able to walk at all for days. Do you think it will all swell up?' Her voice held a ghoulish note and Holly couldn't help laughing.

'It's no laughing matter, they are most poisonous,' exclaimed Jacqueline, putting on her glasses to study the foot.

Christian came back with the young man from the beach bar, who carried a small bottle and some cotton wool.

'No problem,' said the young man, who was dark as a South Sea Islander. His teeth when he smiled were like white almonds in his tanned face. 'All we do, mademoiselle, is to anoint.' He dabbed Miranda's foot with an expert hand. 'And again when she goes to bed tonight, madame.'

A respectful glance at Jacqueline.

'In a few days you will see the thorns all working to the surface. If you use this liquid the foot will not fester. Please,' with a bow which looked very comical from someone wearing nothing but the briefest trunks, 'do me the honour to keep the bottle.'

Exclamations of gratitude from Jacqueline, a large tip from Christian, relief from Holly and giggles from Miranda.

'I thought I'd have a crutch,' she said, hopping away.

Jacqueline gave an exaggerated sigh.

'What courage. She is so like her grandfather.'

Christian, opening his newspaper, did not disagree.

Holly said nothing. She rubbed oil on her legs. Like Miranda, and the boys who worked at the beaches, she was tanned a dark, shining brown and could sit in the sun for hours without danger of burning. She was feeling so happy at present that Jacqueline harping on Miranda's inherited French traits, her plaintive request for the parasol to be moved a fraction, merely amused her. Holly had realised in the last few days that Jacqueline had no intention of opening up the subject of Miranda with her. Her hostess was biding her time. Possibly she'd been advised to do nothing until after the party, the date of which had begun to loom closer. Holly could imagine Christian and Paul, and a lawyer for all she knew, earnestly advising Jacqueline on the wisdom of not upsetting herself. And Jacqueline's resigned agreement. Much Holly cared. She could now afford to be generous. It was a quite strange sensation, intense, joyful, to know that the pain had stopped. She hadn't realised how intense it had been until it was over. She could look into the future now without dread – all because of a few short words of Mike Armstrong's.

Drinking her iced coffee, Holly said tentatively, 'Madame St Martin, I've been wondering. Would you think it rude if I asked whether one of my friends might come to your party? His name is Michael Armstrong, and he is going to be in Provence this week. I told him all about your celebration and he said it sounded wonderful, and that he'd really love to be allowed to come.'

Jacqueline's expression, rather bored at the beach now, brightened.

'An Englishman? A friend of yours from London? Of course you may ask him. I shall be delighted to meet him.'

'It's very kind of you to invite a stranger.'

'Nobody is a stranger who's a friend of my grandchild,' said Jacqueline expansively.

She, too, was feeling generous.

They talked for a while and the subject of the party came up, of course. Ever an opportunist, Jacqueline asked Holly if she would help with the lists, and 'one or two little errands'.

'I know Paul is wonderful and doing everything he can with the arrangements, and of course Christian is paying,' a little laugh, 'but there are things a hostess must do. I have to go through the lists again

112

very carefully. The invitations are going out this week, and I *know* I have forgotten two or three people. You could be such a help, Holly. I'd also be glad if you could see Céline César for me. At the Poterie Artisanale. You know her, I take it?'

Yes, said Holly, she had met Céline. And would be glad to do anything to help with the party.

On the drive back to the hotel for lunch, Jacqueline, surprisingly animated for an invalid, gave Holly what she called 'two commissions for today'. One was to visit Céline that afternoon.

'You understand that I must have my siesta,' said Jacqueline.

The other was to drive to Paul's house to collect the invitation lists.

'So annoying. He took them yesterday to check through them and this morning rang me from Nice. He won't be back until late tonight.'

'He is making some of the most important arrangements for the party, chère,' said Christian disapprovingly.

Jacqueline shrugged.

'Of course. But I can't do without my lists and he's left them at his house. There's always a key to the house at the hotel. Holly, Christian will lend you the car. Don't forget to drive on the right!'

Holly's heart sank. She had been avoiding Paul since he had bitterly offended her by saying that she was setting Miranda against her grandparents. And she could not forget those violent kisses. She did not want to risk seeing him alone.

'Are you sure he won't be back, Madame St Martin?'

'No, he will not,' was the impatient repy. 'He

113

is dining with some friends in Nice. I would ask François to go, but Paul makes such a drama if I use his precious people for anything but their hotel work.'

After lunch, Miranda went to the pool with a number of her friends, and Holly walked to the pottery. She found Céline seated in the shade by the open windows painting a tiny cup. The French girl looked up.

'How are the preparations for the party going?'

'That's why I'm here. Madame St Martin asked me to give you this – it's a sort of sketch of where the flowers might go. But she says of course you must have a free hand. She told me you're superb with flowers. I'm quoting!'

'I'm not bad if I'm allowed to spend some money,' admitted Céline with a laugh. 'Thank you. I think I'll lend the hotel some of my biggest pots. I made some as big as we are. They'll look very good filled with the tallest roses. Actually, they were ordered by the town hall but the mayor changed his mind and bought some old bronze lions instead. I was rather cross. One of the lions is the most hideous shape, poor animal.'

'How lovely everything you make is,' said Holly, as Céline continued to paint a greenish-white passion flower in the base of the cup. Holly bent to examine a tea pot decorated with figures.

'I like your shepherd and shepherdess.'

'You'll see their flock marching across the milk jug.'

The shepherdess on the tea-pot wore the Provençal peasant costume, the striped red and white skirt.

'I wish girls here still dressed like that,' Holly said.

'Oh, so do I. Now we're the same all over the world. Jeans and T-shirts. So dull.'

Céline paused, her brush in her hand.

'Imagine, at the beginning of the nineteenth century, village girls in clothes like that were out on the hills with the sheep. Guarding them against the wolves.'

'Wolves!'

'Yes, indeed, they used to come out of the forest to hunt for a juicy sheep or two. The shepherds had a special warning cry, "Au loup! Au loup!" Mustn't it have been terrifying? They believed you must never look the wolf in the eyes if it came near. Its eyes had power and if you looked, you froze.'

Seeing Holly's fascinated expression, Céline added mischievously, 'I know men like that. Is it why they used to call men wolves in America?'

Holly wandered about admiring the many pieces of exquisite pottery. Propped on a shelf was the plate decorated with Miranda's dancing figure under the mushroom umbrella.

'There it is! Has it been fired? How much do I owe you for it?'

Céline put it into her hand.

'A gift.'

'But I couldn't.'

'But you must! I shall be offended if you refuse.'

Holly demurred, Céline insisted. The plate was carefully packed. 'I'm very very glad you like it and think it resembles her. Of course it must be yours.'

Walking back through the village, Holly thought of Céline's generosity and wondered what special thing she could send her from England. Then

115

another thought came into her mind. There had been sympathy in Céline's expressive eyes. She was sure the French girl had heard about the St Martins wanting to keep Miranda. It seemed that in Vanergues everybody heard everything. Céline obviously believed that Holly would go back to England without her stepdaughter.

Thank God that wasn't true, thought Holly. Anxiety had run through her life now for days like a poisoned stream but at last it had dried up.

Early in the evening she set off to drive Christian's elderly car to Paul's house. She had been surprised when Paul had told her some time before that he didn't live at the Rossignols but had a house ten kilometres away on the edge of the forest. They'd talked about it on the night they had had supper at Chez les Pêcheurs. Paul said he preferred to live at a distance, and Holly remembered that he'd been amused when she told him that the English expression was not to 'live over the shop'. They had been friends then . . .

On the journey in the dusk, she began to feel nervous at the thought of driving to his house. She wanted to go, and yet she didn't. A person's home was so much part of them and, although she and he were estranged, she couldn't *not* be interested and even slightly excited. Jacqueline had given her meticulous instructions, and she drove away from the village, taking a road which led into the hills.

Vanergues was built on one of a series of hills, each steeper than the last, which eventually led to the foothills of the Alps. The land fell deeply near the gorge of the river, and the frowning country was dramatic in sunlight, but in the growing darkness it seemed lonely and ominous. Reaching the valley, then driving steadily up a steep incline, the road entered the fringes of a pine forest. She could smell the resinous scent through the open windows of the car.

This was a country of scents: lavender and thyme, rosemary and fennel. Great bushes of tea roses, and the heavy scent of the night lilies which always reminded her of Paul.

There, at last, were the pillars which Jacqueline had described, on either side of an iron gate propped open by the big white rock. Holly turned into the drive. The garden appeared to be nothing but a jungle of shrubs covered with flowers – it didn't look, she thought, as if Paul had done any gardening in his life. It was beautiful but it was certainly wild. Holly gave a sudden exclamation. An animal dashed straight in front of the car, missing it by inches, snaking low and vanishing into the undergrowth. It was blackish brown with a long tail and a black and white face as dramatic as a badger's. A polecat. The reason she recognised the creature – she'd never seen one before – was because Miranda had recently shown her a picture in a French natural history book of Jacqueline's. 'We might see one. They live in the forest, and they've clever as foxes.'

The headlights shone on an old stone house, one-storeyed, with the usual Provençal tiled roof. Below the roof the walls had been painted a long time ago with garlands of lilies. Like many similar wall paintings on the houses in Vanergues, the flowers were sadly faded. They had turned into the ghosts of lilies now.

Holly switched off the engine and the night silence

filled with a curious noise. It wasn't the familiar sewing-machine whirr of cicadas but a steady croak, croak, croak, a chorus of frogs. First one croaked, then another answered, and then, after a duet, they were joined by an entire frog orchestra.

Holly crossed the drive, went to the front door, fitted in the key and opened the door, groping for a light. She found herself, not in a hall, but a very large, spacious room which apparently ran the full length of the house. There were windows on three sides overlooking the tangled garden, and a fireplace big enough to sit inside. Supporting the ceiling and surrounding the fireplace were great, uneven beams the size of the trees from which they had been hewn hundreds of years before. Unlike Tudor beams in England, these were not black but an unpainted silver grey.

On the far side of the room hung a large painting in glowing emerald, purple and yellow, and when Holly went to look at it she recognised it as a painting by Alain Tessier who had once owned the Rossignols. How different it had looked then, untamed, an old house in a rough rosemary-filled piece of the rocky landscape.

'Do people leave something of themselves in their houses,' she wondered, 'as women leave a trail of scent occasionally?' She looked round with curiosity and a little pain. This was Paul's home. She tried to think herself into its atmosphere, to capture something of him. But the house was mute; it was not her friend and would tell her nothing.

A sound, louder than the chorus of frogs, suddenly began outside the house, steadily growing – it was rain. She went to the window to look out, but it was impossible to see anything through the streams of water already running down the panes. How loud it sounded, as if the rainy season in the tropics had started. Holly thought, 'I shall be drowned when I run out to the car.'

She realised now the significance of this afternoon's glaring white sky. After she'd left Céline she had noticed for the first time since she and Miranda had arrived in Vanergues that the sun had actually disappeared. It was startling to see how everything immediately changed. The colours of the houses were dull, the air was cool, all the lazy pleasure and desire for shade disappeared. Even the doves on the roof vanished. And all through the afternoon the only thing shining from the white sky was a kind of dazzle.

Now the rain beat against the windows as if it was never going to stop. She must find Jacqueline's lists and brave the storm, she thought.

Jacqueline had told her that the lists were certain to be found on Paul's desk.

'He's so methodical, I've never known that man lose anything. They'll be obvious at once. Probably under the paperweight I gave him.'

'He never loses anything,' thought Holly. 'Except my love.'

She saw an olive-wood desk in a corner of the room, with leather folders and letters on it. Sure enough, under a square glass paperweight, was a packet of papers in Jacqueline's old-fashioned writing and violet ink. Holly knew that writing very well. For years it was all she *had* known of her, those 'sincere greetings' on the French birthday cards with their metallic lettering.

As she picked up the papers and carefully put them into her shoulder bag, a voice suddenly called: 'François? Is that you?'

Holly gave a violent start. She'd heard neither a car nor the front door.

She felt a wave of sheer dismay. Nothing would have persuaded her to come here if she had known there was the least risk of meeting Paul. Most particularly in his own home. She stood stock still, her eyes widened, and couldn't manage a word as he came into the house, slamming the front door against the rain. He stared at her in surprise.

'What on earth are you doing here? Did Jacqueline send you?'

'Yes, instead of François. She didn't think you wanted her to ask him. Sorry.'

He raised his eyebrows.

'It's perfectly all right.'

'She said you'd be in Nice all evening,' said Holly, stupidly repeating, 'Sorry.'

She made a move to leave.

'Why are you apologising, Holly? Did you find her precious lists on my desk?'

'Yes. I've got them, but do you still want them?'

'Of course not. I've been through them and done all I can. But Jacqueline hasn't; she'll remember some old friend of Christian's from his schooldays, I'm sure. That's up to her.'

He undid his dark raincoat and shook it on to the stone floor. It was very wet and so was his hair.

As he turned to hang up his coat, for some reason the back of his head, with raindrops shining on his black hair, gave her a little pang.

He turned round and said with an edge of mock-

120

ery, 'It's no good doing up your jacket in that determined way. You can't go yet. It's raining too hard.'

'Oh, but —'

'But you parked Christian's car too far from the front door. I've no intention of letting you drown. I already saved you from a watery grave once, remember?'

'A muddy grave last time,' she said, managing to laugh.

'That's right. So let's have a drink and be comfortable. The house is cold. Rain always does that. Shall we have a fire?'

He crossed the room to where she was standing near the fireplace, and put a match to a high pile of twigs in the grate. They flamed up, spitting and crackling and he stood watching them. The wavering light, first bright, then shadowed, shone on his tanned face and thick, dark hair, on his straight nose and the rounded, determined chin. 'I wish you were ugly,' she thought. 'I wish you weren't so devastating to look at.' She had never known a man like that before. Male beauty unnerved her.

'I have to watch the fire for a bit. If the logs don't catch there's the boring task of fetching more dry twigs and beginning again. Come and get warm,' he said, pulling a stool inside the inglenook.

Holly sat down, and in her turn watched the fire. A small log began to flame.

'Do you like fires, Holly?'

'I love them. They're so alive.'

'So are you.'

It was a careless compliment, casual, off-hand even, but something in her heart seemed to melt, something icy and hard. 'Why am I being so cold,' she thought. 'I'm going to keep Miranda, he can't hurt me any more. So why not just be happy, as I *am* happy with him – or was, until all this trouble began between us. How dreary I must have looked just now when he came in and I just glared at him.'

With a strong effort, she pushed Anne-Marie's ugly story from her mind. 'I *won't* think about it,' she thought. 'I won't let her spoil things.' For now, Holly determined to forget everything, and simply be happy.

She smiled at him suddenly and he smiled back at her. Very thoughtfully.

He mixed them some white wine with black-currant liqueur in a drink called Kir, and sat down near her to watch the fire. The rain went on beating in waves against the windows. It was like being under the sea. They were cut off from other people, free of ties and troubles; firelight and solitude and the wild rain kept them together.

'What a rich house you have, Paul,' she said, looking about. 'I had no idea.'

'You didn't think I bought it, did you?'

'Jacqueline said something about you inheriting it. That sounds rather rich, too.'

'Money in the family? That sort of thing? No, Holly, the owner wasn't any relation of mine. He was my godfather.'

Throwing another log on to the fire, he told her about the house. Like the Rossignols, he said, it used to be a farm and its owner had great stretches of land round here. But by the time his godfather bought it just after the war, it was falling into decay. His godfather had fought with the French partisans, and been wounded. When he came home, he and his local friends, all of them partisans who'd fought together, made a group and banded together to help rebuild the house.

'When they'd finished tiling a roof or rebuilding a wall, my godfather gave a party. He swore the parties cost more than if he'd employed a local builder,' said Paul, 'but they had enormous fun. My godfather was a comedian; he made people laugh. I once saw a friend of his literally staggering out of the room with stomach-ache from laughter. He liked to do unexpected things, too, he had a very impulsive streak in him. You'd understand that, Holly, being impulsive yourself. It was an impulse that decided him to leave me his house. I was pretty staggered.'

'Were your family amazed too?'

'Not my father. He denies it but I'm pretty sure he knew. He's a man who can keep secrets.'

'Your parents are still alive, are they, Paul?'

'Happily, yes. Our home is in Aix-en-Provence. It's a beautiful place, Holly, it's called "the city of fountains", there are fountains in almost every street. And I'm sure you know Cézanne lived there and kept painting that favourite mountain of his. I must take you to Aix.'

It was the sort of invitation a man makes if he likes you, she thought. How he'd changed. He was warm as firelight. He was the man who'd kissed her when they were bathed in the scent of the lilies. They seemed to have stepped backwards. But how could they?

'Don't look at me in that charming way, Holly, or I'll forget what I'm talking about.'

'Your parents.'

'Everybody must tell you what a good listener you are. Here goes, then. My parents had some money when they were young, but the war ruined them. My father also fought in the Resistance, the Maquis, they named it. Those are the low bushes which grow all over the hills where they were in hiding. The war took everything from my father but his life. When peace came, my parents were dreadfully poor. They scraped up what they could to buy a small vegetable shop. I used to work in the shop after school. Often I went to market in the dawn with my father to buy the vegetables and fruit. That's why, you see, I'm good at getting up early.'

'And an expert on fruit and veg?'

'Pretty good, even now.'

He was more relaxed than he had been for weeks with her as he sat talking of his boyhood. It had been hard. There was a time when his father injured his back, foolishly trying to stop his van which had begun to run downhill – the brakes had failed. He had to go to hospital, and Paul and his mother had had to take over everything, the marketing, the shop, the accounts. There had been no school for Paul for a long time. Then his father recovered. Eventually Paul's godfather managed to afford to help Paul to go to Aix University. And after that he had started to train for work in an hotel.

'I remember you told me you came to London. What happened next?'

'I worked in various hotels along the coast. As a porter, in the kitchens and the offices. I think I've done almost every job in an hotel except, of course, being chef. For that you must be an artist. I finally landed up at the Rossignols which is the end of this boring story. It's your fault, for asking to hear it.'

'I liked it.'

'That's kind,' he said, laughing.

'What happened next?'

'Now Holly, do you really want to hear? Oh, very well. I started working for Christian as junior manager. My godfather died and left me this house; he also left me some money, and I bought shares from the St Martins. And more shares later when Christian actually admitted that running the Rossignols alone was too much for him. I think he was quite glad that I was around. He had never had a son to – *oh damn, I'm so sorry!*'

He leaned towards her.

'How could I have made such a mistake?'

'But it's true. Robert wasn't a son to them.'

It seemed natural to talk about Robert. She told him how she and Robert had met when her mother was ill, and how good he'd been to her. Robert's loss of his wife and her own had been a close bond between them.

'He was never really like that again. Not so concerned, so coming-forward, so – so real. Do you know what I mean?'

'Yes, I do. But aren't there friends who are only at their best in the bad times? It doesn't mean they are not valuable, Holly. It is just that it takes unhappiness and trouble to show them at their true worth.'

His words struck a momentary chill. She'd pushed away, because she was safe now, the fear which Paul himself had brought and which recently had darkened her life. Now it was gone and she simply abandoned herself to liking, almost loving, this

125

fascinating companion. But those words had a reverse side.

'It takes unhappiness to show them at their true worth,' could mean, 'It takes unhappiness for somebody to show his real self.' It had shown her a different Paul.

'Was your marriage a disillusion, Holly? I've sometimes thought so.'

'I suppose it was. You see, I did need Robert very much after my mother died. And I believed he needed me. So he did, for Miranda of course, but I'd thought I was going to fill the dreadful void in his life after he lost Sally. I thought I'd be allowed to share his work in some way. He knew that at univerity they all said I was quite a good researcher; I enjoyed digging about discovering things. I had this romantic idea that he was going to take Miranda and me with him when he went abroad, and he'd send me off to ferret away in libraries, or take notes if he was watching archeological digs or preparations for undersea exploration or whatever he worked on. That was the marvellous thing about his books, Paul. It meant going so far to search for such curious things. Sally suited him. *She* went on trips without him. Her newspaper sent her to Australia, Japan and the States. I had no career, I simply ran the house and looked after Miranda. After we married I began to realise he had turned into a loner. Maybe he was one anyway. If I took his arm when we were walking, he used to say, "Do you mind if I swing free?" '

She stopped. 'Why did I tell that?'

'I'm glad you did.'

She met his eyes and he was looking at her with a curious, almost strange look. She had the feeling that

126

something important would happen, something which could change both their lives. She had a surge of love and hope.

But he said only that it was getting late and still raining and he must give her something to eat. Would she come into the kitchen and he'd make an omelette. The spell was broken.

During supper he told her about his friend Margot who lived nearby and came in to look after the house, shopping for him, cleaning, polishing the floors 'far too well', and occasionally, if he invited friends round, cooking a meal.

'I bet people envy you Margot.'

'They do. I've had some loaded remarks from Jacqueline who thinks she should work at the Rossignols. But Margot is very independent, hotel work wouldn't suit her at all.'

'She likes to choose the person she works for, and come and go as she pleases, and it must be somebody she likes.'

'Perhaps that's it. She's so good at everything that she could have the pick of any of the other houses round here. Locally they call her "the pearl". She's very aware of her talents and she needs special treatment,' he finished ruefully.

'You have to be very nice to her!'

'More than that. Postcards every blessed time I go away. Presents from any country I happen to visit. German apple cake. Spanish leather belts. Thank heaven I remembered an English cardigan. There'd be a definite look in her eye if I forgot. It's remembering that look which makes me dash into the shops before I catch my plane.'

'I don't believe a word you're saying! You're as

127

fond of her as she is of you. That's obvious.'

He gave her an amusing look.

'What's obvious is that *you* are a romantic English girl. And one that I fear is going to get very wet,' he added, fetching an umbrella.

The rain still poured as they ran out into the dark, pulling open the car door and climbing hastily in. They had been quick, but were still both drenched.

On the drive back Holly lay and watched the wiper vainly flicking the streams of water from the windscreen – to and fro, to and fro.

'You realise when it rains here it can go on for at least three days. What will you do, stuck indoors in the bad weather?'

'Lots of things. There are all the postcards I bought in the village the day we arrived, for instance. I haven't written a single one. Then there's a dress I'm making for Miranda. Not that she needs it with all the dresses her grandmother has bought her – but I want to finish it just the same.'

'Holly – I've been wondering. Do you think you could help Jacqueline? With the invitations, for instance. She's fretting about them and you know how tired she gets. It would be kind of you.'

'Of course, I'd be glad to.'

Even as she impulsively spoke, a doubt came to her. Was Paul testing her, trying to discover what she felt about Jacqueline? All evening they hadn't once discussed the trouble, but now he seemed to expect her to refuse to help and to say something against the St Martins. She'd said bitter enough things in the past . . .

Holly pushed the suspicion aside. Why shouldn't she do something for Jacqueline, even begin to like her now the lady could no longer succeed in taking Miranda away?

When he stopped under the trees they heard the rain hammering loudly down on the roof. It was as cosy in the car as it had been by the fire: warm and intimate, a square of safety in the heart of the streaming night.

Holly didn't move for a while. She wanted him to kiss her. For a few hours they had been close friends, they had been as close as people can be who have not embraced. She didn't want to leave him without being kissed. He was the man she was in love with. She longed to be in his arms.

He bent forward to look out.

'No sign of letting up. We'd better run for it. Are you ready, little one?'

He might have been speaking to Miranda.

As they ran across the terrace through a storm of rain he put his arm round her so that they could go faster and almost lifted her off her feet. At the door he pushed her into the dry safety of the hall.

'Goodnight, Holly. And sleep well.'

It was still raining the next morning, though not as heavily as the night before. The skies, however, were a dark, uniform London grey and Miranda looked at them irritably. There was no sign of any of her friends. Nothing Holly suggested — drawing? reading? — would do. Dragging down the stairs into a hall darkened by the bad weather, Miranda met her grandfather who was leaving to drive to Grasse to buy some special scent for his wife. He invited the child to go with him.

Slightly cheered at the prospect of any kind of action, Miranda went up to get her yellow raincoat. She returned to the hall buttoned to the chin with the hood fastened round her face. Her grandfather was also raincoated, scarved and muffled against the rain. Holly smiled inwardly. The couple, elderly man and child, looked ready to go trawling in the North Sea.

Holly spent the morning as she'd described to Paul, writing postcards to friends and finishing the hem of Miranda's candy-striped dress. By the time she went downstairs, a watery sun had begun to shine and the garden and the terrace were steaming.

The grey sky was steadily breaking up and turning into wide lakes of blue. Clouds were white and fluffy, moving across the sky like galleons. Within an hour the flags on the terrace were dry and the flowers, the very air, seemed to sparkle.

Unable to resist the rain-washed countryside, Holly went out on to the terrace to look at the freshly green vineyards, the sky, the fields. Far away the mist was clearing from the mountains. They were like beauties wearing thin shawls which were slipping from their ample shoulders.

'Hi, there!'

Standing by the hotel entrance with a broad grin was Mike Armstrong.

Holly rushed to greet him. They hugged and he gave her a kiss. In typical Armstrong fashion he immediately said that, even if they could fit him in, he wouldn't be staying at the Rossignols.

'I've booked at a place in Nice. Very reasonable, special terms really, and I've fixed to have use of the landlord's bath. Not bad, eh? I say, Petal, this is one hell of a place. I should think the bill here costs a pretty packet.'

'Happily, we won't be asked to pay,' she said, laughing.

'Count yourself lucky.'

She ordered coffee, and sat down with him on a bench which was already dry in the sunshine.

When she looked directly at him, the pleasure in her face died.

'You didn't just come for fun. What's happened?'

'I'm afraid the news isn't good, Petal. I saw the barrister again.'

'Oh, God.'

'Don't look like that. Not here.'

He looked round.

'Somebody might be watching us. It's all not as straightforward as it first looked. He's a top flight man, I promise. I had a meeting with him yesterday, and he went into it all thoroughly, as much as he could, of course, based on the information I've given him so far. He's been making enquiries about cases like this. He said one of the troubles is your age.'

'*What do you mean?*'

'He described you as still a girl. It seems that the courts in the UK or in France would both raise that. Almost certainly they'd come down on the side of the grandparents. Responsible people of mature age and so forth. Giving the child a settled home.'

'A settled home when she's been with me for all this —!'

'Don't burst out like that, Holly. Wait a minute and let me tell you. And, who knows, somebody might hear you. We need poker faces, I promise. This is a tough one to crack and we've got to be

131

clever, so listen as quietly as you can. We'll talk as much as you like later. I'll drive you to Nice.'

'Well?'

She could scarcely bear to listen.

He made a grimace, like a man probing for a thorn in a bleeding hand.

'To repeat myself. The problem of your age. And the big question being that you might marry again.'

'Of course I won't.'

'You say that, Petal, but you're twenty-five and extremely attractive. They'd only have to look at you. He said that, compared to the grandparents, you're simply too young. If you *did* marry again and had kids of your own, they might change your attitude to Miranda. Don't start bursting out again, for Pete's sake! I know it isn't true but they wouldn't know. How could they? All they have to go on are facts. Cold facts. The long and the short of it is that you're no blood relation. Only the stepmother.'

6

There was a great wall made of fountains. Not one or a group of three or four but a line of enormous jets shooting and falling, shooting and falling with a wonderful steady roar. At the top of the jets the water seemed to throw itself into the air with joy.

'I counted them,' said Mike. 'A hundred and forty-two.'

It was early afternoon and Nice was full of sauntering crowds. How untroubled they all looked, thought Holly, and she envied every one of them.

Mike stopped at a large pavement café within sight of the fountains, ordered some ices, and told her in detail about his meeting yesterday with the lawyer. Holly mustn't get too depressed or think that there was no hope. You could never be certain of the outcome in cases like this.

'So Miranda has become "a case" has she?'

'Petal, be realistic. There's obviously going to be some sort of fight with these French relatives, so there is nothing for it but to brace up.'

He spoke in his flat, businesslike way and patted her hand. Privately, he thought she looked haunted. It was pathetic to see her making an effort, saying how grateful she was for him coming to France to see her.

'That's nothing. I'll be wheeling and dealing over here, you know me! By the by, did you manage to fix an invite for me to go to the shindig at the posh hotel?'

She managed a pale smile.

'You're very keen, Mike. I should imagine it's going to be boring, all those smart French people knowing each other. Why do you want to come so specially?'

'Now why do you think? Where there's money there's trade. Well? Am I asked.'

'Jacqueline St Martin said yes.'

'Great.'

He finished his ice. A thought struck him.

'You don't look so good, Petal. We could change our plans, you know. Make a dash for it? I don't mind forgetting the party, things are lively in London just now, and we could leave tonight if you like. On the late plane. After I've popped in to see our Nice agent.'

The sudden offer, out of the blue, was most unselfish and most unlike him. He rarely did such things, preferring to be kindly when it was also useful. Holly was touched. Oh, how she wished she could say yes.

'I'm afraid I can't leave until after the party. I've got to stay.'

'Who says?' demanded Mike. 'You haven't *got* to do anything.'

'Because Paul's making me,' she thought.

'Jacqueline St Martin's health isn't all that good. She's pretty delicate. I simply daren't take Miranda away before the big night. If her grandchild left now it could easily make Jacqueline ill.'

He scratched his nose and looked at her ruminatively. She believed what she said, or she was too strung up to disbelieve it. Intensely suspicious, and given to tactics himself, he thought it sounded a cooked-up reason to keep the child in France. Holly was too soft. Well, wasn't that what he fancied about her?

He let the subject drop, however, for there was no point in trying to dissuade somebody whose mind was so obviously made up.

They left the café and strolled through the blazing streets. Nice, thought Mike, was an entertaining place. It reminded him, in its buzz and smartness, of a smaller Paris which happened to be by the Mediterranean. He took Holly's arm and they crossed the road on to the enormous Promenade des Anglais. They leaned over the railings and looked down at the beach.

There was none of the golden sand of Cannes or Juan here. The Nice beaches, steeply shelving, were stony, white and grey. Sunbathers lay stretched on towels, pinned to the shingle by the sun. Children shouted and played. The sea, with its floor of stones, was a wonderful translucent blue, and children shouted and played along its shallows, while windsurfers, their sails the colours of the rainbow, drifted gently by. Mike put his arm round Holly's thin shoulders and pulled her close. He wanted to kiss her.

'Glad I'm here, then?'

'Very.'

'Did I remember to tell you that I adore you?'

'Oh Mike, please.'

'I don't see why not,' he said, unabashed. He burst out laughing.

When he drove her back to Vanergues, he sat with her in the car for a moment before she returned to the hotel. He looked at her with what Holly called his business face. The ingenuous grin was gone. He looked tough.

'Let's re-cap, Petal. Since you've decided you've got to stay on, you must play a very cool hand. We haven't heard from our man what he thinks the next move should be. While we're waiting, we must keep them guessing. *Don't* show you're worried. Refuse to talk about things. Look, and stay, cool. Didn't you tell me Madame seems to be avoiding the subject? Good. You do the same. And don't talk to *anybody* but me about it. OK?'

During the following days, Holly tried to do exactly what he had told her. It was very hard, and sometimes nearly impossible. She had to look cheerful, pleasant and unsuspicious. She had to appear natural when she felt more unnatural than she'd ever done in her life. To meet Jacqueline's sharp blue gaze with an unconcerned smile. To seem in good spirits and not to feel her heart would crack when Miranda hugged her or merrily talked about Richmond and the autumn term at school. Sometimes the effort of all this made Holly literally feel sick.

The only thing she did not have to worry over was seeing Paul alone. He was very taken up with preparations for the party, and almost never came into the private gardens.

The days passed in their accustomed pattern. Holly swam or sunbathed, listening to the doves. She went into the village and met Mike for drinks. She lunched with Miranda on the terrace. Life shone with a gloss of luxury and was filled with Mediterranean light. Every one of her thoughts was dark.

And Paul was not just part of the darkness but its centre. He'd been kind and even tender to her at his house the other night, simply because he knew he was going to win. Now she was sure that Anne-Marie's story was true. Miranda was his child. He wasn't making preparations only for the St Martins' party — but to keep Miranda in France.

Despite her state of mind, Holly decided that she would offer to help Jacqueline. Being with her a good deal would make the risk of a showdown neither worse nor better. Jacqueline agreed so promptly that Holly, suspecting Paul more, thought he'd been put up to the idea. Jacqueline was clearly a woman who, as she described it, 'likes people running about after me'. She piled tasks on to Holly, including three hundred invitations which had to be filled in by hand — and the envelope hand written as well since it was more polite — and all the acceptances kept in a book and recorded every day after the post had come. There were also the acceptances made by telephone.

Early in the week of the party, which was to be on Saturday, she suddenly asked Holly to go and see Paul.

'He wants to see who has accepted so far,' said Jacqueline, shuffling her lists into a messy bundle.

Holly simply couldn't think of how to refuse. She wanted to snap, 'Can't someone else go? Why can't *you*?' But Jacqueline was sighing, preparatory to going upstairs for one of her rests. Taking the papers in silence, Holly left the study and went up the stairs.

She knocked.

'*Entrez.*'

She opened the door and went into the room. Mike's advice rang in her head. 'For Pete's sake don't show you're worried. And refuse to talk about it.'

Paul was at his desk, the afternoon sun's deep gold slanting through the window on to his face. He looked very tired. But when he saw her his whole face changed. He gave her a smile of welcome.

'I haven't seen you for days. Is Jacqueline working you into the ground? I know you wrote all the invitations, I saw that pretty handwriting of yours. It really is good of you to take on such a chore.'

'She asked me to bring you these.'

She put the acceptances in front of him.

Her face, her voice, struck him in surprise.

'Sit down, Holly. You don't have to run off just yet, do you?'

She was so nervous that she could feel her heart beating.

'You're very quiet,' he said, and again gave her the smile which in the past she'd thought seemed to envelope her, to promise something, to pull her close. She knew none of those things was true. She didn't even pretend to return it.

'We haven't talked about Miranda either, have we?' he said gently. 'Is that what's making you look so serious? We should have discussed it the other night at my house, but you didn't seem to want to. So I didn't either.'

'I don't wish to talk about it at all.'

He was puzzled.

'But we must. After the party's over we must sit down and —'

'I've told you. I won't talk about it *with you*.'

Her voice was so harsh that the affectionate expression in his face vanished. He was annoyed.

'What do you mean? I've told you that it's better not to go into it all with Jacqueline. Certainly not before the party, she's in quite a state already. We don't want a family row, Holly.'

She was angry, frightened and excited. Her resolves were forgotten, her face flooded with colour.

'So I'm expected to sit down and let you get away with it? Of course you don't want Jacqueline involved, she has to be protected from everything, doesn't she? Anyway, what's she got to do with it? The one really out to get Miranda is you.'

He was flabbergasted.

'*Me*? Why should I want the child?'

'Because you're her father.'

'What in hell are you talking about?'

'You deny it, then?'

'Deny it? Deny something so – so ludicrous. How can I be Miranda's father, for God's sake? She's your husband's child. I never met her until this summer. Stop talking wild rubbish.'

'I don't believe you,' she said fiercely. 'I don't believe a word you say and I wish I'd never set eyes on you.'

'I can agree with that if you're willing to accept any filthy story that's put about. Who told you this?'

Even through the red mist of anger it sounded to her as if he spoke the truth.

'How could I be Miranda's father?' he repeated harshly. 'It's impossible.'

'Somebody said you and Sally St Martin had an affair.'

139

'And Miranda was the result. Perfect.'

He looked at her with a face as hard as flint and she thought: 'He's a stranger, what do I know about him? Nothing. Nothing. I was mad to fall in love with him.'

'Why did you believe that disgusting story?'

He was now as angry as she.

'It could be true.'

'Oh thanks. Thanks very much. And this "somebody" who told you? You prefer to believe them than to ask me, and give me the chance to deny it? It's obvious that you think me perfectly capable of seducing the girl who was to marry into the family I love. As I said, thanks.'

'*I don't know you.*'

'You certainly don't. Who told you this vicious rubbish?'

She said nothing.

'Oh, let's be loyal,' he said with scalding sarcasm. 'You show little loyalty to me in believing it. Now you defend whoever made the mischief. Of course it was Anne-Marie, I recognise her style. Nobody can trust her as far as they can throw her. She'll say anything; scandal's her meat and drink. It amuses her to make trouble. Now please go. I don't want to talk to you.'

'*You* don't want to talk to me!' cried Holly, her cheeks still flaming. 'You deny the story, but how do I know who's speaking the truth? This place is full of lies. All I know is that you're against me, that you plot and scheme to steal Miranda and, as far as I'm concerned, you could very well be her father, it's just the sort of horrible –'

'*Stop that!*'

140

He sprang up and went across the room to a desk. He pulled out papers and letters, dropping some on the floor. Finally he extracted one from a drawer. He threw it towards her on the table.

'It would have been nice, it would have been very nice, if you'd paid me the compliment of believing the truth when I speak it. But since you accept any damned thing against me and require evidence, which sickens me, read that. It's from Sally. I kept it because it touched me, it was such a happy letter. I never imagined I'd need it for something like this.'

The letter shook in Holly's hand. She recognised the bold, overlarge writing which had been scrawled in some of Robert's books.

'My dear Paul, It was such fun to meet you at Vanergues in the spring and remiss of me not to write to thank you for looking after us beautifully, when everything was distinctly rough! But after we got home the wedding was such a rush, and then we went to Washington, only a five day honeymoon in Nantucket, and since then, work, work, work. But I've finally got myself together, and want to thank you for being *really* kind. Provence was a disaster except for you. I also want to tell you the merry news, which is that we're expecting a baby. I'm knocked out about it, isn't it wonderful? I can't tell you how happy I am. Robert said he knows you'd be pleased, specially as I nicknamed you My One French Friend, so . . .'

Holly couldn't read any more. The voice in the letter was so vibrant, the feeling of the past so strong. She put it carefully down on the table.

'I'm sorry.'

'So I should think.'

141

'Please forgive me.'

He gave a kind of shrug but said nothing.

'I suppose I shouldn't have believed it.'

'No. You shouldn't.'

He was not going to accept her apology. He put her cruelly in the wrong about everything, when all the time she was only fighting to keep Miranda. And trying not to love this angry stranger.

She left the room quickly, shutting the door.

When he was alone, he picked up the letter and looked at it. The writing was bold and hasty, the words rushed carelessly across the page, filled with joyful friendliness. He folded the letter, and its happiness lay inside it like a flower. It had been rich and fragrant once, and it was dried now, and browned, and beginning to fall to dust.

Holly didn't see him again that day or the next.

The preparations for the party were growing steadily and there was much delivering from vans and telephone calls and more and more acceptances for Holly's records. Miranda was intrigued by the coming and going, and often came to look for Holly to report what was happening and coax her to come and watch. There was the big ballroom, which was to be made ready for a dinner for over two hundred guests; there were the barns, arranged to take the overflow. Ceilings were looped with blue-striped awnings, like the tents in a medieval film. Miranda and her friends could no longer splash in the swimming pool, for sanded and waxed planks had been fixed across it. It was destined to be a dance floor.

Each morning Miranda spent most of her breakfast time hanging over the balcony to report the news.

'A big van's arrived. I do believe it's champagne.'

'Look, Holly, all those little gold chairs.'

The hotel bustled, Miranda commented, and Provence was looking at its loveliest. Since the rainstorms, the air was washed so clean that the country seemed made of crystal. There was a scent of herbs and roses. The busyness and pre-occupation, and more still the beauty round her seemed to mock Holly's sombre thoughts. Her confrontation with Paul had left her shaken. She'd misjudged him and was bitterly sorry. But how did that change anything? He still meant to get Miranda.

Mike turned up at the Rossignols now and then, and Holly introduced him to Jacqueline, with whom he was so egregious that Holly wished he would stop. When she said said so later all he did was grin.

'What a girl you are. You'd never make a poker player.'

He was not very often with Holly, since he was using his time to meet the biggest estate agents along the coast. He went to Cannes, to Juan les Pins and to Antibes. Various meetings which were fixed by his Nice agent were promising, and there was the sign of one juicy deal, as he called it. He took Holly out to an inexpensive restaurant on the port of Nice to celebrate. Although she saw less than she'd hoped of him, he was so matter-of-fact, optimistic and level-headed that she was dismayed when he said he must go back to London unexpectedly. She felt her moral support was leaving her.

'Something's come up at the office which they can't handle without me. I shall take the chance to see our barrister while I'm in London. I rang him this morning. I told him he must think positively,' said Mike, laughing. 'So when I get back I can tell you how things are. The party is on Saturday, right?'

'But are you sure you want to come back again? Another journey, merely for the wedding anniversary of people you scarcely know,' said Holly doubtfully. She wanted him to come back. But she didn't want to be a burden to him. She felt indebted enough.

'Of course I want to come. Didn't somebody say "the rich are different", Petal? Nothing's going to stop me joining in the fun.'

She missed him when he was gone. He was her one ally. But a small yet vital problem now occupied both her thoughts and Miranda's: what were they going to wear for the party?

Miranda was very decided in refusing Holly's suggestion that Jacqueline might like to choose the dress. *No*, said Miranda. Holly must take her to find one. And Holly needed a new one too, didn't she? The child was quite irritable, and Holly agreed. They took the long, hot bus journey to Nice twice, looking for new dresses. They visited large shops and small. The expeditions were exhausting and Miranda grew tired and cross. Holly wanted them to wear the best dresses they'd brought with them, and forget the idea of new ones. But at the end of the second afternoon, in a boutique in a narrow street in the old Italian part of Nice, they found what they wanted.

It was a pretty little shop, and when they entered it the woman who served them was fat, motherly, and as Italian as the old pink houses outside in the square. Miranda discovered just the dress she wanted: short white taffeta dotted with big blobs of blue, pink and yellow. The skirt had a double frill, and Holly thought her stepdaughter looked like a dancer in costume as a lollipop. Finding something for Holly proved to be more difficult, for Holly hadn't forgotten the barrister's remark that she was too young. She tried on dress after dress, in the hope of looking more mature.

Finally it was Miranda who decided for her.

'You've just got to have this one. She looks terrific, doesn't she, signora?'

She appealed to the Italian lady who pressed plump hands together, saying it was the best, the very best, and Holly looked perfect.

Holly looked at herself in the glass; at the layers of green and white tulle, the thin shoulder straps made of white silk flowers. She thought it made her look younger, not older. But Miranda was determined.

The great day dawned at last, and telegrams and flowers began to arrive before breakfast. Jacqueline, up hours earlier than usual, sent for Holly and Miranda. They found her downstairs, elegant in embroidered white lawn, (Holly recognised one of the lovely, if girlish, dresses from Haut de la Pinède). Jacqueline took them to her study. The room was already so crammed with flowers and piled with trays full of letters, cards and telegrams that the girls could scarcely edge inside. It was like trying to enter a star's dressing-room after she'd won a Hollywood Oscar.

Jacqueline stood at the door, surveying the spoils with a complacent smile.

'How kind people are. How very kind.'

145

She bent forward to re-arrange a four-foot long red rose.

Christian appeared.

'Now, chère, you must not tire yourself. You are going to need all your strength for tonight,' he said reproachfully.

'Yes, you're right, I do feel a little strung up,' she agreed, moving away. Clearly in the direction of her chaise longue.

A sense of excitement ran through the hotel and communicated itself to the guests staying at the Rossignols. They were interested and amused at the movement and bustle, huge bouquets bobbing up to the entrance every ten minutes, more cables, telephones shrilling. When the St Martins made one of their rare public appearances, to have their lunch on the terrace, there was a scatter of applause.

At twilight, the lamps in the cypresses and olive trees, strung like pearl necklaces, sprang into light. A subdued hum could be heard in passages and on staircases, the clink of glasses, shifting of tables. With so much fascinating activity, Holly was sure Miranda would be under everybody's feet. She went to find her. To her surprise, Miranda wasn't watching it all. She was on the terrace, kicking her heels against a chair, staring into space.

'Shall we begin to get ready, Miranda?'

'If you like.'

They went to their room. Miranda had a bath and Holly washed her hair, muffling her in a towel and rubbing energetically. Miranda tugged away.

'Do keep still, darling,' Holly said.

'Oh, leave off, it's *dry*.'

Holly's heart sank. She had not heard that voice

since Miranda had been so rude to her grandparents, pretending not to understand French. It was both sulky and disagreeable.

In silence Miranda put on her underclothes and went to the bed where Holly had spread out the new dress. Miranda pulled it on, didn't wait for Holly to do up the buttons, and flounced over to the long mirror.

She looked at herself.

'I hate it.'

'Miranda, don't be silly.'

'I hate it,' she repeated, tugging off the dress. She threw it on to the bed, went to her chest of drawers and began messing about with a pile of sundresses, finally picking out the sundress Holly had made. She put this on and marched back to the glass.

Holly watched in amazement. Miranda's cheeks were red, her mouth a thin line. She glared at herself. Holly was mystified. Miranda was behaving very badly, yet somehow she couldn't be angry with her.

'Do you like your sundress better?' she asked gently.

'No I don't and it's got a dirty mark where the twins pushed me into the hedge.'

Miranda peeled off the sundress, threw it beside her new one, rushed across the room and flung herself weeping into Holly's arms. Holly hugged her in silence. What was wrong? She scarcely recognised this temperamental, difficult child. Was she the same person as the sunny companion who'd been with her in Richmond for five years?

'What is it, darling? What's the matter. If you really dislike the lollipop dress, you don't have to wear it. Let's see if we can find something you like better.'

147

Crying hard, Miranda brought out, 'I'm stupid. Stupid. I don't want Pierrette to look nicer than me.'

'She won't. She might look just as nice, and you'd be glad, surely, as you're so fond of her.'

'No, I'm not, she's French,' was the sobbing reply.

'But you're French. Half French, anyway. You can't start hating half of yourself.'

'I'm not French, I'm English like you and Mike and everybody at home. I am English, aren't I?'

'Darling, of course you are!'

Holly wondered what quarrel with Pierrette had brought on a rush of youthful patriotism.

The sobs were beginning to quieten, Miranda had arrived at the sniffing stage. Holly brushed long strands of hair from the child's eyes.

Taking her by the shoulders, she said, smiling, 'What about putting some cold water on your eyes?'

'They're all right. Is my nose red?'

'I'm afraid so.'

'Let's see.'

Miranda marched to the mirror again and studied herself.

'Well, I like it red.'

She stayed still when Holly helped her to put on the lollipop dress, to fasten its tiny pearl buttons and arrange its short, frilled skirts. Looking at herself, Miranda said reluctantly, 'OK.'

Then she saw that Holly was putting on the green and white tulle.

'Oh, you're *beautiful!*'

For a moment it seemed as if the tears would start again, but with a loud sniff she ran from the bedroom, with a flick of polka-dotted frills.

Holly finished dressing and went slowly out into

the corridor. The hotel was in a turmoil when she came into the hall. Maids hurried by with boxes of candles. Waiters carried big trays of glasses. Out in the St Martins' garden there were all kinds of lights shining. Céline had floodlit great pots of flowers; the fountain basin was circled with little red oil lamps. There were large and small pools of light everywhere, the necklaced trees, the candles burning in the still air. One pencil of floodlight caught an alcove on the Rossignols wall where a statue of Saint Réparate stood, bowered with leaves, the nightingale on her wrist.

Moving among her guests, receiving kisses and congratulations, was Jacqueline. She wore a diamond necklace and a magnificent dress of palest pink taffeta with skirts trailing in a slight train. Her air was smiling and regal as she leaned on her husband's arm. Seeing Holly, she gave a slow, queenly nod.

Holly wondered if Mike had yet arrived. He had telephoned the hotel to say he would be rather late. She looked round and saw many people she knew. Parents of Miranda's friends. Anne-Marie in the distance – Holly decided to avoid her. And then she caught sight of Paul on the other side of the garden, talking to the head wine waiter, a burly man in dark blue wearing the ribbon and silver medal of office. The waiter nodded and went into the hotel. Paul saw her, and came across the garden.

'Good evening, Holly.'

His voice was cool. She was miserably embarrassed, remembering the scene in his office, but managed to say, 'Everything looks very splendid.'

'Yes, it does. It's Céline. She did the lighting as

well as all the flowers . . . You look very beautiful,'
he added. If it was possible to pay a compliment
unkindly that was what he did. Before she could
reply, he said he could see Céline had just arrived,
and must speak to her. He bowed and left.

As she watched him go, a voice called loudly in
English, 'Petal!'

There was Mike, unfamiliar in a dinner jacket. He
strode over to give her such a smacking kiss that an
elderly French lady nearby raised her eyebrows.

'Did you get my message? I rang from the airport.
Only flew in an hour ago, how's that for good tim-
ing? I say, you look luscious. That's some dress, it
must have cost a million.' He looked her up and
down, and then gazed round with eyes full of interest
in everybody and everything. He fetched two chairs
and sat down beside her.

'What a rich lot, eh, Petal? All these people must
be rolling.'

'Mike, please don't talk so loudly. Many of them
speak extremely good English, you know.'

'So who minds being called rich?'

Something about his attitude to money slightly
repelled Holly. He had once told her there were only
two things in the world to be: either bigger than the
next man or wealthier. 'And I'm short,' he'd added
with a grin.

After sitting for a while looking at the crowd of
guests, he suggested they should go for a walk
round. He took her arm and they made their way
through the gardens to the entrance of the ballroom.
It was filled with tables laid for dinner. All the
candles had been lit, throwing a steady golden
radiance on white lace, silver, and bowls of white
flowers.

150

'Where shall we put ourselves? What about over there just by the big table where they serve the champagne?'

'I'm sorry, Mike. I forgot to tell you that the St Martins have invited me to sit with them.'

He gave a whistle.

'The Captain's table, eh? Wish I was joining you. Not to worry, I shall have to find myself another girl. Have you got any likely candidates?'

Looking at her sideways, he smiled.

'Don't look so bothered. You must know by now that I don't need help to find a pretty woman *or* a good business prospect.' He looked across the room and suddenly called out, 'Hi, Paul. Could we have a word?'

Paul had been looking for Holly, and came up to say that he was taking her to the St Martins. But before he finished speaking, Mike buttonholed him and began to talk about property in London. Paul listened with unconcealed impatience and when Mike finally stopped, he said abruptly, yes, well, they'd talk about it some other time but now he had come to take Holly to supper.

'Sure, sure, bear her away. See you later, Petal. Unless the other girl won't let me go!'

Paul accompanied her across the ballroom which was now filling with people, who crowded round the place charts or bent to look at place cards. As they threaded their way between the tables, friends greeted him and he cordially replied. She was intensely conscious both of his presence beside her and of the fact that he didn't speak a word to her. They finally came to the table where the St Martins were already seated.

151

'What a glorious party, Paul!' cried Jacqueline, 'Even better than we imagined, isn't it, Christian? So perfectly organised, everything as it should be. Superb! And all because of you.'

As they sat down, Paul said it was the work of everybody at the Rossignols with the addition of a good many willing hands from the village. It was a united effort to show what the St Martins meant to Vanergues.

'And the town hall is joining in. I hear the Mayor is giving a reception for you both tomorrow,' he said teasingly.

While Christian talked boringly about the Mayor, Holly looked round for Miranda. A big table was set for eight not far off, and she saw Miranda busy talking to her friends. She looked happy enough and Holly felt relieved. But why *wouldn't* Miranda enjoy this evening? Holly herself had never been to such a glittering occasion. Voices filled the ballroom with a steady roar, waiters hurried by with silver trays of wonderful food. The diffused light of the hundreds of candles shone on bare brown shoulders, jewelled necklaces, deep blue chiffons, lemon or black silks of the women, the white dinner jackets of the men. Candlelight transformed people into figures of a more romantic century. The scene had the quality of a dream.

Jacqueline now commanded the attention of all three of them. She must tell Paul – Holly, listen now! – Christian, do you remember? – about the day of her wedding. Did Christian recall her gown sewn with brilliants which at the last moment was discovered to be three centimetres too long? It was impossible to walk (let alone up the cathedral steps!)

and she had had to stand on a table while the dress-maker shortened it. Oh! she felt so nervous. Had she ever told Holly about Christian's speech at the wedding luncheon? It had been so witty. And, changing the subject neatly to keep Paul's interest, did Paul remember when he had first come to the Rossignols as a child?

'My dear Jacqueline, I was twenty-three!'

'As I said, a child. Then when your dear godfather, the great hero of the Resistance, died . . .'

She dabbed her eyes with a lace handkerchief.

To distract and comfort her, Christian began to talk about the menu and for a while Jacqueline abandoned reminiscences as they discussed the various dishes to be served. They commented on them, thought Holly, like people at an exhibition talking about the paintings. Certainly it was the most delicious meal Holly had ever eaten. Everything was light and delicate, the servings quite small. No sooner had one dish finished than another, as tiny and fine, was placed in front of them. There was Parma ham so thin it was transparent, served with little fragments of Charentais melon, then came fresh salmon pressed flat, with a fluffy sauce faintly tasting of basil. There were little tender steaks with black cherries, salad of avocado and slivers of raw mushrooms and, for dessert, a miniature soufflé à la Grand Marnier. Holly marvelled. How could Jean Du Loup make *four hundred* soufflés? But there they were, delicious little things, each in its individual dish, being whisked from table to table.

Eating with an appetite surprising for an invalid, Jacqueline again demanded an audience. She talked sentimentally but amusingly of the past. She would

153

never forget the dreadful bedroom they'd been given on their honeymoon. It was just after the Liberation and of course everything was in chaos. They'd stayed at a château which had once belonged to a seventeenth-century family said to be worse than the Borgias. Oh, the bedroom! She could swear it had been a prison. Then – did Paul remember the night the Baron came to dine at the Rossignols and the roof was leaking, it dripped all over her hair just after she'd returned from the coiffeur? Anybody watching the quartet during dinner would have thought them a close, united family, with Jacqueline the beloved mother, Paul and Holly the devoted children . . .

Holly was glad to laugh at Jacqueline's stories. Paul did not avoid speaking to her and, when he did so, he was quite pleasant, but she could hear in his voice that he remembered the scene between them. She could see it in his handsome face as well. How can you still be offended when *you* plan to injure *me*, she thought. She concentrated on her hostess, laughing at Jacqueline's conceited little jokes, and respectfully listening to Christian St Martin re-telling anecdotes that she had heard before.

'Your dress is charming, Holly,' remarked Jacqueline, after a good many compliments about her own. 'Do I recognise St Laurent?'

'Oh no, I bought it at a boutique in Nice,' said Holly, slightly laughing. 'Miranda and I both bought dresses there.'

'Tiens, I could have sworn it was Yves St Laurent,' said Jacqueline, losing interest. She gazed across the shimmering room. 'Where is the little one? I haven't seen her yet this evening.'

'Over at the children's table. Shall I fetch her?' said Paul.

'Gracious, no, let her finish her meal. So bad for the digestion to be disturbed. I shall embrace her later,' said Jacqueline.

Christian enquired if his wife could manage another marron glacé. Paul spoke of the vintage champagne, had it been to Jacqueline's liking? 'How they spoil her,' thought Holly. 'They never stop giving her her own way.' And with an inward shudder she thought, 'I am being forced to do the same.'

While she drank her coffee, she wondered how soon it would be polite to get away and look for Mike.

'Would you like to dance?'

Paul's invitation was cool enough, and Holly was about to make an excuse when Jacqueline said, 'Of course you must both dance. I shall dance with you too, Paul, but first with Christian. Imagine dancing on top of a swimming pool. What a clever idea of yours.'

'It was Céline's.'

'You're too modest. I know quite well that *you* thought of it.'

Holly stood up, and Paul walked with her out of the ballroom into the warm gardens where more candles burned and more small lamps shone.

On a small stage by the dance floor a group was playing reggae. There were two guitarists, two drummers, and a young man playing the flute. Paul led her to the floor as a West Indian voice began to sing to a haunting beat:

Why must I cry these tears from my eyes,
Makin' believe you love me only . . .

Holly loved to dance and almost never did. Now and then in London Mike took her to a disco, and while people danced he merely sat and talked. How often she'd simply longed to dance. All during her marriage Robert had never taken her dancing. It didn't interest him. It was six years ago since, at University during one term, she'd danced almost every night.

Now as they went on to the floor, her green and white tulle skirts swayed. The music embraced and released her, and she began to move with a sensuous grace, half smiling. She did not see Paul looking at her. She thought, 'You don't want to be with me so I shall pretend to be alone,' and danced away from him to the sound of the singer's rich, dark voice telling of the sadness of the heart. When the music ended and a drum rolled, she was some distance from him.

Mike appeared.

'There you are. And hello again,' to Paul who came to join them. 'I'm here to steal your partner. We Brits have to stick together, you know.'

With a murmur, Paul left them.

'Damn,' said Mike, 'He disappeared rather fast. I want to get going about that new hotel they're building. He really should fly over to take a look at it. Ah well, I must catch him later. Come and have coffee and I'll tell you how sexy you look.'

They returned to the St Martins' garden where, quick at such things, Mike captured a bench in a far corner just as a couple vacated it.

'Now I've got you to myself. Shall I get you a raspberry ice? I can recommend them. Coffee? Vino?'

156

'Not a thing, thank you. The meal was delicious, wasn't it?'

'Three star. And I found a girl to sup with. She wasn't half bad – Anne-Marie something, a friend of Paul's. Does he fancy her? I rather did.'

'I have no idea. Do you think she's attractive?'

'Sure, but not as much as you. And rather hard, like most Frenchwomen.'

'Oh Mike, don't pin labels on people.'

'Why not? Labels are a big help. You know where you are with a label or two, and the one I'm pinning on you tonight is "sexy".'

He sipped his wine, then said, 'I saw the lawyer yesterday. He's going to take the case.'

Her heart fell like a stone.

'How awful it sounds.'

'Oh, I don't know. It isn't all bad on our side, you know. We have to think positively. Remember? I said that to the lawyer and he actually agreed. It certainly won't be a walkover for the grandparents. He said custody is such a tricky one. All based on what's best for the child, of course, the right atmosphere, the stable home and so on. Miranda could be asked what *she* feels about it all. You'd hate that, I expect.'

'I'd loathe it.'

Her voice shook.

'You're getting into a tizz again. Don't. There's something I want to say to you, Petal, which could make a big difference to your chances. The lawyer agrees.'

'What? *Anything*!'

'Marry me.'

It was so utterly unexpected, and his way of

speaking it so bland that for a minute Holly was dumbfounded.

'Is the case as hopeless as all that?' she bunglingly managed at last.

'What do you mean? You must know how I feel. I suggested we could live together last winter, remember? I could have moved in then. You just laughed and acted as if I was kidding, but I wasn't. Marry me, Petal. I'll make a good husband. You know I think you're super, and we'll make a good team. And think how it alters the problem of Miranda. *We'll* give her the stable home, see?'

She didn't know whether to laugh or cry. It was true that some months before Mike had pounced on her one evening at Richmond, and been difficult to handle. He'd been rather drunk, and wanted to make love, and kept saying she was the one for him and they ought to live together. Holly had coped without hurting his feelings too much. Thinking it over afterwards, she had come to the conclusion that her money, and Miranda's, and the pleasant house were all pluses to practical Mike. But what should she think now? Mike never did anything for nothing. Having seen the Rossignols and, guessing that Miranda was going to be an heiress one day, he'd discerned further advantages, including the wealthy people with whom he'd be able to do business. Yet she liked him, despite all this. And he was kind to her.

'I'm very touched, Mike. And grateful,' she said in a low voice, 'but I couldn't marry you.'

'What's to stop you?'

'Dear Mike. I don't happen to love you.'

He actually laughed.

158

'Of course you do. Look how well we get on.'

The tone was still confident, but when she looked up, his eyes weren't.

'No, Mike, I don't love you. I'm very fond of you, and grateful, but I couldn't marry you.'

She had never seen him at a loss before. His freckled face was blank. Then, with a visible effort, he returned to being the man she knew.

'Ah well, can't win them all. I dare say I shall ask again; one doesn't make a sale at the first attempt. Shall we circulate? I really ought to have another go at Paul Deslauriers. Perhaps you could give me a hand?'

As if to say – you owe me that.

They walked across the gardens, and he kept a sharp lookout for Paul. Business had taken over again, thought Holly. He was tough, and if he was hurt he'd never show it.

Making royal progress through the masses of people, and still accepting congratulations, came the St Martins. Jacqueline bowed graciously to Mike, and then said to Holly that she had forgotten to show her the gift Christian had chosen for their anniversary.

'It went out of my mind during supper. I was too emotional,' said Jacqueline. She held out a plump arm. Round her wrist a diamond band winked with blue and white fire. She moved her hand to make the stones blaze more.

'They've always been my favourites. Christian said diamonds suit my colouring.'

While Holly dutifully admired the bracelet, she saw, with dismay, that Mike was talking to Christian. He had not been more than briefly introduced,

159

in this country which retained its formalities, but now he leaned back, legs apart, exuding thick-skinned good humour. The conversation was in French, clumsy and confident on Mike's part. Still pretending to look at the bracelet, Holly tensed, waiting for Mike to offend.

'I'd like a chat with you, monsieur, about some hotel properties in London. Paul —' Mike was too fast with Christian names — 'Paul is keen on the possibilities outside the capital, Sussex or Surrey, but London is the place for your kind of top-flight hotel and what I have in mind . . .'

The elderly man listened in silence. Like Paul earlier this evening, he disliked business at this celebration. It offended him, and his lined face, handsome as a carved figurehead on an old ship, was grim. Holly knew, in any case, that he had no wish for a hotel in England. Mike was in full flood, making mistakes in French and laughingly extricating himself, when Paul appeared. He caught the conversation.

'I'm afraid we can't allow any of this,' he said with decision. 'Tonight is not for business, is that not so, Christian?'

'True. Tonight is for the family,' said Christian. There was relief in his face as he turned to his wife, saying she must give him the dance she had promised. With a cold bow to Mike, he walked away with Jacqueline on his arm.

Mike was not a man to recognise a snub. He'd caught sight of Anne-Marie, voluptuous in clinging white, and strode over to join her, beginning a laughing conversation. Paul watched him for a moment.

Then he said quietly, 'Call off your English bull-dog, please.'

'What Mike does is nothing to do with me.'

He raised his eyebrows.

'I gathered he was here because you asked Jacqueline to invite him. He is your friend, surely? Tell him he can come to the office in the morning.'

'Tell him yourself,' snapped Holly, knowing she sounded like a rude child. But her feelings were raw. 'I take no responsibility for Mike. He's always like that about his work. He goes at things like a bull at a gate.'

Paul said drily, 'I call him a bulldog, you a bull. Both descriptions seem to apply. But I am sure you have some influence over him, whatever you say.'

With one of those French bows, he moved away.

Holly stood alone. Mike, still flirting with Anne-Marie, stopped a passing waiter, took two glasses of champagne, put one in the French girl's hand and whispered something to her. She smiled provocatively. 'Perhaps,' thought Holly, 'now I've refused him, he is going to desert me for the rest of the evening. Well, I don't blame him.'

In the distance, the reggae music began again. She had a wave of such loneliness. She felt infinitely lonelier here among all these elegant strangers in the candlelight and the warm Mediterranean night than she had ever felt in London as part of the indifferent millions living in a great city. She was homesick for her own house, for the shabby sitting room and the window wide on to the garden, and the roses unfurling their curled petals, and Miranda begging for garden picnics.

She thought, 'I'll find Miranda.' Talking to

Miranda would feel like home. She looked round for her.

She began to walk through the gardens, a slender figure in green and white, saying a quiet 'excuse me' as she threaded her way among the vivacious throngs, searching for one little English girl. In the ballroom it was the second service, people were having supper and waiters were still moving about with loaded silver trays. But the table where the children had sat was now freshly re-laid and occupied by a number of young men and girls gaily talking to the accompaniment of popping champagne corks.

Holly went back into the gardens. During a pause in the music, she heard children's voices, and almost ran round the corner by the rosemary hedge. There they were, the children, dancing. The twins were jiving energetically. One little girl wearing a wreath of daisies was doing a kind of polka. Two larger girls were dancing together. There was Sophie, the eldest and the leader, dancing alone.

'Sophie,' called Holly from the edge of the floor. 'Is Miranda around?'

To the music's beat, Sophie swayed towards Holly.

'She was with us at supper but I haven't seen her for ages. Pierrette went to look for her.'

'Where's Pierrette now?'

'I'll ask the others.'

She danced over to the rest of the children. There was a vigorous shaking of heads. She returned to Holly.

'No luck. Guy said he's seen Pierrette who hasn't found her yet. Maybe they've both gone upstairs.'

Giving Holly a dreamy smile, Sophie began to circle to the music.

Holly went round the dance floor. She looked in corners, on benches, among crowds seated on the grass. She began to feel just slightly bothered. Where *was* Miranda? The most sociable of creatures who enjoyed being with her friends, and most of all with Pierrette. Of course the answer must be that she and Pierrette had gone off to play somewhere. It wouldn't be hard to find them.

For the next twenty minutes Holly searched. She went up to her bedroom, thinking perhaps Miranda had had another fit of temperament and crossly decided to go to bed. In their room one lamp was lit, the beds beautifully folded down. There wasn't a trace of the child. Not a shoe, not an open drawer. It was clear that Miranda hadn't entered the room since they had left early that evening.

As she returned down the stairs, Holly was really worried. The two children must be somewhere! The old porter François was on duty in the hall. Had he seen the children? No, madame, not at all. Observing her expression, he asked kindly if he could fetch Monsieur Deslauriers?

Half unwilling, obscurely comforted, Holly agreed.

A minute later Paul came down the corridor, walking fast.

'François says you want me.'

'I can't find Miranda or Pierrette.'

His face had been concerned. It relaxed.

'My dear Holly, in this crush. That's ridiculous!'

Without realising what she was doing, she put her hand on his arm. It was as if a small electric shock

163

went between them.

'Paul. I'm scared. I've looked everywhere. Miranda's nowhere in the gardens. Nor in our room. I found the other children and they said they haven't seen her since supper. Pierrette went looking for her. Now I can't find Pierrette either. They must be together. But where?'

He stood for a moment in thought.

'Look. Don't tell the St Martins. Here's what we'll do. First we'll go to all the places you've looked, and check them again. Don't say anything more to the children either, we don't want to alarm them. Then, when we've both looked everywhere separately, we'll meet here in –' he looked at his watch – 'quarter of an hour.'

They parted.

Holly went through the whole anxious journey again, from one room noisy with laughter and gleaming with candlelight to the next. Twice in the gardens she saw Paul in the distance.

In quarter of an hour she was back on the terrace. The sound of the party went on, with its music and the dark melancholy voice of the singer.

Paul came out of the hotel and joined her.

'I found Pierrette.'

'*What did she say?*'

'She's been looking for Miranda since supper. Poor child, she was crying. I told her there was nothing to worry about and sent her to join the others.'

They looked at each other.

'She's run away,' he said.

'Paul! Why are you so certain?'

'Because I asked the housekeeper to help. She and a chambermaid have been all over the hotel. You and I have combed the gardens and the ballroom. And Pierrette has been looking for more than an hour.'

He went on gravely, 'Has she ever run away before?'

'Never.'

Holly looked at him in panic. Miranda was lost. Miranda had run off somewhere, into the village. She was hiding in some dark garden, or even further away still in the countryside. *Why* had she gone? *Where?* How could they even begin to find her?'

'Oh what am I going to do?'

He took her hand and gripped it.

'We'll find her together. She can't have gone far. She must be in the village.'

'You can't come with me. They'd miss you.'

'Do you think I'd let you do this alone? Come along. There isn't a moment to lose.'

Vanergues was asleep. Most of the lights in the old houses were out, the tourists were gone long ago. As Paul and Holly hurried from the hotel, the noise of the party gradually died down. They reached the square. It was empty and silent, the café chairs stacked, the shops shuttered. Céline's pottery was closed and lonely.

Together they went from street to street. They climbed and descended worn flights of steps, crossed alleys between walls, peered into the porch of the locked church. Now and then Holly called. 'Miranda!'

But nobody answered. No child's voice replied. A cat ran across their path and once there was a crack of wings as some doves wheeled from one roof to another. High up on the top storey of an old house a TV began to chatter, with the quick intense voice of a French newscaster giving the midnight news.

They went down the stone stairway to the elaborate gardens of the town hall, looked in the playground and under the olive trees. Finally, they returned to the square. Here, the silence was filled with the trickle of the fountain. But no child sat, crying or defiant, waiting to be found.

Paul stopped still.

'Think, Holly. Try to think. You know how her mind works. Where might she go? Not even a child of nine runs off without some idea of a destination. When people do things on impulse they always have an idea. *Think*.'

Holly tried. She went through all the places she'd visited with Miranda, and those to which Miranda had been taken by other people. But they were all, except for the bus journeys to Nice, miles away in a car. Miranda had been to Grasse, to Antibes, to Vence and St Tropez. Places a child could never reach, never find . . .

And then she remembered. She had told Miranda

166

about her walk to the Manosque farm, that day Paul had followed to warn her about the swamp. Miranda had been interested.

'Is it very dangerous? How beastly. I wish I'd seen it. Where exactly did you walk?'

'*Paul, I think I know where she's gone.*'

Even while she talked, they began to run to the car. He set off fast, driving out of the village and along the road until he reached the turning up the hill. Neither spoke as the car bumped over stones, rounded the twisting corners. At last they reached the place where the fields spread out, mile after mile towards the mountains.

A huge moon shone in a wash of blue.

'Did you tell her about the swamp? Are you *sure*?'

'Certain. I said you'd told me how dangerous it was and how somebody had been drowned there.'

They were moving at a run across great moonlit spaces and suddenly Holly gave a cry.

Ahead of them, quite far off, was a sort of hump in the meadow which looked at first like a rock, but as they came nearer turned into a figure. Holly had never run so fast in her life. As she rushed towards her, she was afraid Miranda would spring up and run away. The figure didn't stir.

Holly reached her first and fell on her knees.

'Oh Miranda, oh Miranda.'

Paul, behind her, said with strange gentleness, 'Didn't you know how frightened Holly would be?'

Miranda began to weep. She collapsed on the ground, her face in the grass, hysterically sobbing and as Holly pulled her into her arms Miranda almost screamed,

'I won't live in France, I won't, I won't, I won't live

167

with Grandmère. Pierrette keeps talking about it and then after supper, oh, it was awful! Grandmère came to find me and she said I was a French child now, and would stay here for ever. And I won't. How can I when you're my mother? If she tries to make me I'll run further next time, and nobody will find me.'

The dreadful sobs sounded as if she were choking.

Holly stroked the bent head.

'Darling, why didn't you tell me? How did you hear? What did you hear?'

'Pierrette was in the garden and they thought she wasn't listening and Grandmère told her mother,' came the weeping reply, 'about keeping me always. Pierrette's mother said afterwards how happy I'd be staying in France always. But I'm not. I'm miserable, miserable.'

Above the figure pressed against her, Holly met Paul's eyes. He leaned down and gently took Miranda in his arms as if she were a baby. Worn out with crying she said, 'Don't be cross with me.'

'My dear child.'

There was a break in his voice.

They walked back across the meadow. The moon had turned it to silver and small flowers brushed against their feet, springing back into place as they walked on. There was the hoot of a hunting owl. A faint wind sighed.

On the drive home Miranda lay in Holly's lap, now and then giving the shuddering gasp of somebody who has cried for too long.

'Are they all very angry?' she timidly asked at last.

'Nobody knows but us.'

When they drove into the village, Paul parked the

car and turned off the engine. The noise of the party seemed to have grown louder.

'We'll creep in across the terrace. Shall I carry you, little one?'

'I can walk, thank you.'

They slipped into the hotel and Holly said, 'I'll take her upstairs.'

He watched them go, a thin figure in diaphanous green and white, a weary, small figure in grass-stained taffeta.

When they were in the bedroom Miranda just stood, arms hanging. Every line of her figure was desolate.

'Come and sit on the bed with me and we'll talk.'

'What about?' said the child drearily.

But she climbed up on Holly's bed and leaned against her, as a dog does with its master. Holly smoothed the hair from her dark, anxious eyes.

'Tell me, darling. Were you horrid to your grand-parents, pretending to forget French and everything, because of me?'

Silence.

'What's so terrible about living in this lovely place?'

'It isn't lovely if you aren't here.'

'But your granny loves you.'

'She means to. But she sort of pretends. Like she pretends to be ill. I don't want to talk about it.'

The voice wavered.

Holly paused, her arm closely round the thin figure beside her. Then she said slowly, 'Suppose I said I'd never leave you?'

Miranda spoke in that new, timid voice. 'Could you make them give me up?'

169

'I shouldn't think so, darling. They're your grand-parents. Don't pull away like that, just listen. I *promise* we'll stay together. I'll stay here. We can sell the Richmond house, and I'll come and live in Vanergues too. What do you say to that? When my French gets really good I might get a job here at the hotel. The point is that I'll be *with you*. Not in England. Not on the other side of the sea. With you. Always.'

Miranda had fixed her eyes on Holly. There was hope and a fear of hoping in her face.

Holly went on talking. She made things sound matter of fact and easy, even rather comic. She described selling the house, the fun of packing their things, the idea of a new school in France, at Pierrette's, of course. When she finally stopped there was a little silence.

Miranda fiddled with the flowered straps of Holly's dress.

'I wouldn't be horrible any more if I had you. I wouldn't run away or anything.'

A long sigh.

'Holly, I so love you.'

'And I love you. Best of all.'

Holly hugged her tightly. Miranda squeaked. She sighed again, climbed down from the bed and kicked off one shoe. It hit the wall.

'You will like it here, won't you? Promise? I suppose it's quite nice really, though I still think Richmond's better.'

'We'll both like it.'

'We could learn to do wind-surfing. Some of them aren't bad at it, but we'd be better.'

'Much better.'

Miranda nodded thoughtfully.

'That dress is a bit of a mess, Miranda darling. Shall we find another? If you want to go back to the party, that is?'

'I think I do. Now.'

Holly washed her stepdaughter's face, brushed her hair and tied the velvet belt of a fresh blue dress. Miraculously Miranda was herself again. She chatted. She hung out of the window to see if she could spy any friends. With a final, 'Oh, how I love you,' she went out of the room. Holly heard her clattering down the stairs.

Some words of a poem came into Holly's mind when she was alone.

> For I have promises to keep
> And miles to go before I sleep.

What a promise she had made just then. To give up all her English life, everything she knew and understood. It would be the same for Miranda. They both had to start again. Knowing, at least, that they were not going to be torn apart. How loud the party sounded when she, too, went down the stairs. But the reggae music was beautiful and she thought she would sit and listen to that. As she came round the rosemary hedge Miranda appeared, hand-in-hand with Pierrette who peered up at Holly from beneath her fringe.

'Pierrette's mother says can I stay with them tonight and we're going on a boat to the island tomorrow early. May I?'

'May I?' repeated Pierrette in imitation, having no idea what the English words meant.

'Of course. What time will you be back?'

'Pierrette's mother said about five. Promise you'll be here.'

Anxiety suddenly re-echoed.

'Now where else would I be? I'll be in the garden and you can tell me all about the island. Which one are you visiting?'

'Sainte Marguerite. That's the big one. Pierrette says we're going to look at the prison where they kept the man in the iron mask, poor thing. See you tomorrow at five, then. OK?'

She grinned, and disappeared, still holding Pierrette's hand.

Beyond the rosemary hedge, near the dance floor and the musicians, was one of the low stone walls, all that remained of the Rossignols' faraway convent past. Along its top were lines of small, glowing red lamps. Holly carefully moved a few, and sat down with the lights on either side of her.

The music was a reprise of the number that had been playing when she danced with Paul.

> Why must I cry these tears from my eyes,
> Makin' believe she loves me only,
> Goodbye to hope, goodbye to love.
> Why must I tread this lonely road,
> Making pretence my heart ain't lonely . . .

'Goodbye to Richmond,' she thought, 'and the syringa, and our next-door friends and school and holidays by the seaside. It is true, I have promises to keep. There's no way out but to come and live here. I suppose people might think that a glorious fate. Perhaps I might learn to love Provence, if it were not for Paul. How long does it take, I wonder, to un-love?'

So many different kinds of love. Hers for Miranda, and Miranda's for her. Jacqueline's greedy love for a grandchild. Even Mike with his eyes on the main chance had offered her a sort of love.

As she sat watching, she noticed a group of smart, elderly people at a table on the lawns. Mike was amongst them, looking thoroughly at home and in deep conversation with some friends of the St Martins whom Holly recognised as the owners of a hotel in Cannes. Her eyes turned to the dancers. She saw a girl with a mass of foxy reddish-gold hair. Anne-Marie was dancing with Paul. Holly didn't want to watch them, but she found she couldn't take her eyes away. They suited each other so well. They were stylish and confident, contained and very, very French. They knew what they wanted, knew how to manage their lives. 'He's quite forgiven her for telling me that old scandal,' she thought, 'so why hasn't he forgiven *me* for believing it?' She couldn't answer, and finally looked away from them.

The drums rolled, the music stopped, Paul and Anne-Marie vaguely clapped. As they returned to some friends, he saw a pale figure sitting on the wall, with a long row of lamps on either side of her.

He went across the floor to Holly.

'How's the little one?'

'Better. Much better. She's gone to spend the night with Pierrette.'

He still looked down at her.

'What did you tell her?'

She said wearily, 'What do you mean, Paul?'

'I mean did you say you'd take her back to England.'

'No. How could I? I didn't say that.'

173

She was afraid he would ask more. He didn't. She waited for him to go. But he moved a few more of the lamps and sat on the wall next to her.

The music began again. Why did it sound so sad?

They listened to the singer for a while and then he said, 'Come for a drive with me.'

'You can't leave the party again.'

'I most certainly can. I've been doing my duty for –' looking at his watch – 'over eight hours. It's time to escape. What do you say?'

He drove her away from Vanergues in silence. It was a different kind of drive now. Anxiety no longer flew above them like a huge, terrifying, black bird. The night wind lifted her hair and she lay back, wishing they could drive all the night through. She didn't care where they were going, or even if the drive was very short. Just being here, knowing Miranda was safe and Paul was by her side was enough. Lovers had thought that since time began. We only want this, they said. Just this short time of bliss, we know it will soon be over, we have no future and no past and all we ask is this little, little time. For a brief moment she was senselessly happy.

He said nothing, his powerful hands on the wheel, his eyes on the road. Finally, 'Guess where we're going.'

'I don't know my way anywhere.'

'You should recognise this road. We're going to the coast. I'd like to look at the sea.'

'I'd quite like to look at it, too.'

'The English always do, don't they? The island people.'

'Yes, we're an island people,' she thought, 'and dangerous things happen to us when you tempt us across the water.'

The road ahead was almost empty. Houses lay in darkness. But when they came into Juan the coloured lights were winking with names like Hollywood, Gentleman Jim's and King Kong. Music came flooding out of the discos. Paul turned on to the beach road.

Here all was deserted and quiet. The busy life of the shore had ended with the sunset. No cars were parked half on the pavement, no bronzed figures padded by, barefoot, carrying plastic dolphins. It might have been deep winter. Yet the air was warm as milk and the moon shone on a sea as flat as glass. The waves broke with a dull, faintly phosphorescent glow.

Parking by Guy's shuttered bar, he took her down the wooden stairway. There was a deck built round the bar. They sat down facing the sea.

Across the moonlit sand, wherever she looked, Holly saw thousands of footprints filled up with shadow, the signs of the day now gone. So many people had been here, and all had vanished now. A single car went by, driving fast, then the silence washed back with the sound of the waves.

'Has he brought me here to talk about Miranda?' she thought. 'Well. It's all settled now though he doesn't know it.' Some of the knots in her heart were loosened. Some never could be.

He picked up a stone and threw it towards the sea.

'You didn't tell me what you said to Miranda after we brought her home.'

'It was all OK,' she said evasively.

'Now how can that be? What did you tell the poor child?'

175

'Why do you particularly want to know?'

She felt exhausted. She didn't know if she could bring herself to tell him about her promise to Miranda. Suppose he tried to dissuade her. He wouldn't succeed; but there had been a kind of truce between them since they had gone to look for Miranda, and she couldn't bear it to be broken.

'Because I'm part of it all, I suppose,' he said.

'You mean because of the St Martins' little empire, as Christian calls it.'

'The little empire is pretty tangled up at present,' he said, after a moment.

'So that's why you ask. Because she's going to inherit some of it eventually.'

He sighed.

'What you're asking *me* is if I want Miranda to remain in France, aren't you? I'm afraid I do. You think that cruel of me but it isn't. You have all your life ahead of you. You're young and strong. You'll have children of your own.'

'Don't start saying her grandparents have a right to her! After what happened tonight I can't bear any more. Later, perhaps. When I feel less raw.'

'I'm sorry. I understand.'

He was silent. Then he said, 'I never told you, but Christian's been under a great strain. The hotels haven't been the big success everybody believes. He bought some land in Spain four years ago, paid too much for it and didn't consult me. It was a disaster.'

'What do you mean?'

'He didn't have all the searches made and it turned out that the land was two kilometres from the flight path of a newly-planned airport.'

He heard her draw a breath.

'Exactly. He had to sell the land and he lost a lot. Naturally the business suffered. But then I inherited my godfather's money, as I told you, and put it into the Rossignols. Later I put in more. One way and another things are better. But he had a terrible shock. We thought he'd be seriously ill. And . . . Jacqueline being so frail . . .'

Holly listened. She had hated the St Martins and now she saw that, selfish as they were, they were old and weak. She understood Jacqueline's desperate longing for a new young life to be joined to theirs.

'You think Miranda will give them something to live for.'

'For Jacqueline, yes. Christian isn't so involved except that it touches her and he can only be happy if she is. In a way, having lost their son, I feel they deserve Miranda. Oh, if you'd heard her talking about the child, Holly, you'd have been sorry for her. She's very pathetic. But what's to be done? Miranda would never agree to stay. Tonight proved that. She would run away again and next time it would be worse. So. You win.'

Holly hesitated. Then spoke in a rush.

'I've told her I shall come and live in France.'

'You've said *what?*'

'That I'll live here. I'll sell the Richmond house. I won't be penniless.'

There was an extraordinary silence.

'You actually promised?'

'Don't try to stop me!' she burst out. 'I *shall* come. Don't say that I can't!'

'My dear Holly, I've just told you that you've won — Miranda would never stay in Provence without you. Now you've solved it all by the most quixotic gesture I've heard in my life.'

'Don't laugh at me. I hate it.'

'I'm not laughing at you.'

She said in a low voice, 'I do love her very much.'

'You don't have to explain that to me,' he said irritably. 'I know exactly how you feel. I actually take the trouble to understand the people I'm fond of. You don't.'

She was too upset to hear anything but the reproach.

'You mean I believed you were her father.'

She shouldn't have said it, it sounded all wrong, but she was worn out.

'Yes I do. I was very angry. You'll say it was nothing but hurt pride but that isn't true. I'm not offended by criticism. I like it. But that! What I couldn't take was that you hadn't given a thought to the kind of man I am. You were capable of getting everything about me utterly wrong.'

'You haven't exactly made things easy for me, have you? How do you imagine I've felt, knowing you were trying to take her from me? I was certain that if they went to the courts – which God forbid – the St Martins would get custody of Miranda. I *am* young. Too young, they'd say.'

There was a pause.

'Now it's settled,' he said. 'By your imagination and generosity. All for the best in the best of all possible worlds, eh, Holly?'

The words were kind. Not the tone. Not at all.

'I had better drive you home.'

'Must we go yet?'

'I think we should.'

'Can't we stay a little longer?'

'What for?'

'Oh, Paul. Don't let's drive home being so cold with each other. I'm deeply sorry I believed that story, but everything was so frightening and so mixed up. I came to France innocently enough. I didn't know what we were walking into.'

'A trap.'

'It seemed like that. I was so terrified of losing her. And I knew you weren't on my side. It's horrible not to have a friend when the going's rough.'

'You have a very good one.'

'Who? Not you, surely?'

She did feel tired.

'I'm talking of somebody much closer. Michael Armstrong.'

'Yes, he's a friend. He really tried to help.'

He said nothing for a moment, then asked if she was cold. She said no, but it wasn't true. There was dew on the wooden deck.

'You say you plan to come and live in France. What about Armstrong?'

'He can come and see us if he wants to. But I don't suppose he will after tonight.'

'What does that mean?'

'I said I won't marry him.'

There was another of his silences.

'Why? Why did you refuse him, Holly?'

'Oh, why do you think! Because I don't want to marry him, of course.'

'You may change your mind. He's clever and already seems very successful. He'll go far. Couldn't you be happy with him?'

'You don't even like him.'

179

'I've no right to criticise your friends. You ought to marry.'

'Well, I shan't,' she said flatly. Why had he bothered to drive her here and why had she wanted to stay? All he did was sit and ask her sharp questions. She shivered.

'You *are* cold.' He leaned over and put a warm hand on her bare shoulder. He gave an exclamation.

'You're freezing. What am I doing, bringing you down here to be chilled to the bone. You're worn out. I must take you home, and you should go to bed and sleep away all your worries. In the meantime, wear this.'

He took off his jacket still warm from his body and wrapped it round her.

Standing up, he pulled her to her feet and into his arms. They began to kiss. He kissed her over and over again, pressing her to him so that every part of them touched. Her heart thudded so hard that she was sure he could feel it. She leaned against him, shutting her eyes.

He let her go.

'*La belle Anglaise*. What are you thinking? That it's disgraceful of me to kiss you, and you want to run away like Miranda?'

He began to pull her to him again, she resisted, but he was too strong.

'You hated me when I kissed you the other day. You were angry with me. It was exciting. You don't think much of me, do you?'

He lifted her chin with his hand and stared down at her.

'I can read your eyes, Holly. You don't trust me.'

'I don't understand you.'

180

'How mournful you look. So pretty. So sad. Has it all been my fault, making you look like that? Was I cruel to try and keep the little girl for her grand-parents' sake?'

'I do understand now. But Paul –'

'What is it, *ma belle?*'

'Please let me go.'

Being near him was making her body behave treacherously; she had begun to tremble. He didn't loose his arms and seemed to ignore the involuntary movements of her thin frame.

'Do we forgive each other, then? I'll forgive you for believing those lies. You must forgive me for hurting that brave English heart.'

'Not so brave. Terrified tonight when she ran away.'

'You needed me then, anyway.'

There was a silence of kisses until they separated, and he looked at her again in the curious blueish light.

'I'm the one who doesn't understand. Not a thing. Here you are in my arms, returning my kisses so passionately, but how can you do that when you don't care for me one bit and I adore you? Yes, it's true, I'm in love with you. And you don't feel a thing.'

'*But I love you.* All the time, even when it was at its worse, oh – my dearest –'

They stood for a long time on the deserted beach and the moon rose in the clear sky, making a watery path on which no foot could tread. Sometimes they murmured broken words. The waves sighed. They'd seen lovers before.

The telephone rang.

'Holly. Did I wake you?'

'Oh no.'

'Did you sleep well?'

She'd been broad awake staring at the sunlight coming in bars through the shutters. It was nearly seven o'clock.

'You don't answer. You slept well?'

'Not at all. Since we said goodnight.'

She heard him laugh. 'Nor I. I suppose I can't persuade you to come out and have breakfast with me on the terrace?'

'You're not here already!'

'Since an hour ago. Could you bear it?'

She washed her tired face with cold water, threw on a sundress and went down through the entrance hall and out on to the terrace. A single table had been laid in a far corner. When Paul saw her, he ran. They met half way, and he kissed her three times, once on each cheek, the third kiss on her mouth.

'Dear love, how wan you look. Come and sit.'

'You look tired, too.'

'We're idiots. I wish I could kiss you properly. I must pull myself together. Strong coffee, that's what we need.'

He thought how delicate she looked: pale, despite her tan, and gentle, and utterly happy. The contrast between her tiredness and her swimming eyes made his heart ache for some strange reason. He was used to deliberately alluring women, and there she sat, smiling and wan and all unconscious of her beauty. A girl in a pink dress.

'I nearly rang you at half-past four but thought it would be cruel to wake you. If I had known you were

182

awake anyway . . . I couldn't remember if I asked you to marry me.'

'Well. I thought you did.'

Her face was as impish as Miranda's.

'Thank God for that. I remembered a lot of things but nothing sensible. Are you *sure* you want to?'

'Oh yes. Please, yes.'

They looked at each other for a while.

'Jacqueline is very bright at half-past six, as she never tires of telling people' he suddenly remarked.

Holly was puzzled.

'Surely you haven't seen them already.'

'Yes I have. I rang and they were already having breakfast. I asked if I could come up.'

'Why in such a hurry to tell them about us, my darling?'

'Not to tell them that, although of course I did later. I wanted to tell them that Miranda ran away last night.'

'*You didn't!*'

'Dear love. Did you think I'd keep it from them to protect them? They had to know. They were horrified. I told the whole story, about how you found she was missing, our search, our decision not to tell them because of upsetting the party. Then I said where we'd found her and the state she was in. I also told Jacqueline that Miranda ran away because of what she'd said to the child last night. About staying in France for good.'

'It must have hurt her, poor thing.'

'It had to be done. I made up my mind about that last night, the moment we realised Miranda was gone. This morning Christian got the point at once. He knew what Jacqueline wanted was impossible.

What kind of life would it be for Miranda, let alone for them, never sure she wouldn't run away again? Capturing a child who wanted to be with someone else. What I didn't mention was your promise to come and live here. Since you and I have changed that a little. Jacqueline,' he went on thoughtfully, 'was upset but she took it surprisingly well. Christian was tough with her. He almost never is, and she didn't have much choice but to behave. Something else came up. It was the moment of truth with a vengeance. Apparently it was the way Jacqueline behaved which estranged Robert. "You don't want to do the same thing again, do you?" he said to her. Poor Jacqueline didn't utter a word.'

'But what did she *do* to Robert?' exclaimed Holly, astonished. 'She seems so proud of him.'

'She was dead against him marrying an English girl. It seems there was an heiress with a family in Nice who owned loads of property, Jacqueline wanted her as a daughter-in-law. When Robert and Sally came here, she did everything she could to separate them. She was unpleasant to Sally and left her on her own so much that I began to take her about. Mother and son argued and talked and finished up having a huge row. Which has been on Jacqueline's conscience ever since.'

Holly gave a long sigh.

'Poor Jacqueline. But she'll still have lots and lots of Miranda, won't she? I mean, we'll be living here all the time and when we're married I'll sell the Richmond house –'

He picked up her hand and absently kissed it.

'How you miss the point, *ma belle*. Why do you think I'm marrying an English girl? To get a home in

184

London, of course. We are definitely *not* selling that pretty house, because the St Martin hotels are going to extend to England. I've started my campaign with Christian, and I already notice glimmers of interest. Particularly when I gave him some rough figures. So, we shall live in both places. Our little girl might go to school in France. School holidays in England? And she could go to University in England, if she works hard. Would that suit? I believe in English all these suggestions of mine are called having one's cake and eating it.'

'What would you call it in France?' she said, laughing.

'Ah. We would call it signs of the practical Gallic soul.'

There was some significant comment in the Rossignols kitchens about the young English lady and Monsieur sitting on the terrace at such an unearthly hour, ordering breakfast and not eating a crumb. Jean du Loup, brilliant chef, himself exhausted by his triumph of last night, said they were simply tired after the celebration. Was that surprising after such a magnificent success? The girls in the kitchen exchanged glances. They knew that two people meeting almost in the dawn, and eating nothing, was romantic.

The doves on the roof cooed all day long, a soporific, soothing noise. After all the noise and movement of the party, the Rossignols was in a spell. Holly sat in the garden, thinking that the nightingales ought to come back. Paul lunched with her, scolded her for her pale face, and sent her off for a siesta.

Punctually at five, Miranda came into the private garden looking for Holly. Jacqueline had not appeared yet. According to Christian she needed repose and yet more repose. Miranda found Holly and Paul alone by the fountain.

She came towards them, carrying an enormous bunch of freckled white and dark red carnations which she put into Holly's lap.

'These are from me with love and hugs.'

'Miranda,' said Paul, 'give me your hand.' He put out his.

She went to him trustfully, and he said in the gentle voice he'd used to her last night.

'Holly's going to come and live in France, isn't she? So as to be with you.'

Miranda gave a toothy smile. Holly could see that she was finding it hard to keep still – when happy, she hopped.

'What would you say,' continued Paul, still grasping the little brown paw, 'if I told you I was going to be part of the family? Holly's very kindly said she'll marry me, and you will be living with us.'

Miranda's large brown eyes grew larger.

'Will you be my stepfather, then?'

'Something like that.'

'Terrific.'

Escaping from the kind hand, she broke into a jig.